LOST BETWEEN HOUSES

DAVID GILMOUR

LOST

a novel

BETWEEN
HOUSES

vintage canada
a division of random house of canada

VINTAGE CANADA EDITION, 2000

Published in Canada by Vintage Canada, a division of Random House of
Canada Limited, in 2000. First published in hardcover in Canada by Random
House Canada, Toronto, in 1999. Distributed by Random House of Canada
Limited, Toronto.

Vintage Canada and colophon are registered trademarks of Random House
of Canada Limited.

Lyrics on p.29 from "Baby It's You," written by B. Bacharach, B. Williams, M.
David

Canadian Cataloguing in Publication Data

Gilmour, David, 1949–
    Lost between houses : a novel

ISBN 0-679-31029-0

I. Title.

ps8563.156l67 2000   c813'.54   c99-932499-3
PR9199.3.G55L67 2000

Text design by Gordon Robertson

Printed and bound in the United States of America

10 9 8 7 6 5 4 3 2 1

Dedicated to my editor, Dennis Lee

and

In memory of my extraordinary mother,
Virginia Logan Wolfe

LOST BETWEEN HOUSES

CHAPTER ONE

T HAT NIGHT my mom took me to dinner at this French restaurant downtown. It was a cosy little place on a back street. The guy came over and spoke to her in English but she answered him in French, giving me a little look just to make sure I was listening. He took us to our usual perch on the second floor. I loved sitting up there, you could see the whole place, the people eating, the waiters gliding around, a pretty girl in the coat-check room. I raised my arm to get the waiter's attention.

"Don't," she whispered. "They have radar. The good ones."

Sure enough the guy, who had his back to us, looked around, saw my mother with her chin on her hand and hurried over. She ordered a martini.

"You know what I was thinking today?" she began. My mother loved getting all dressed up and going out and when she was happy, like she was tonight, she could talk the hind legs off a donkey.

"I was thinking that you should have a party. You're sixteen and you've never had one. And I suddenly realized why." She touched my hand just to make sure I was paying attention.

"You're afraid, no, *afraid* is the wrong word, you're nervous rather, that no one will come. I felt exactly the same way when I was your age. The *shame* of no one coming!"

Her martini arrived and she took a sip, giving it her absolute attention, like she was listening for a very faint sound from the other side of the city.

"Heaven," she went on. "You know where they make marvellous martinis? Italy. There's something about Italy that makes you want to have a martini."

She lit a cigarette.

"So here's what you do. You get all dressed up in your finery. You invite lots and lots of pretty girls, they inevitably give a party a sense of occasion, and you get your best friends to come early. People love parties. I'm not exaggerating, Simon, may God strike me dead, but it's more fun to *give* a good party than to go to one."

She reached over and grabbed her purse and opened it and pulled out her cheque book, flipped it open and extracted a narrow silver pen.

"Just for fun," she said, "let's draw up a list of all the people you'd invite if you *were* going to have a party."

So the two of us sat there throwing down names on the side of the paper tablecloth. Very français that, the paper tablecloth.

The waiter came over.

"Vous avez décidé, Madame?"

"Non, pas encore. Mais dites, encore un, s'il vous plaît," she said, pointing to her martini glass.

"Comme vous voulez, Madame."

"You never say, un autre," she whispered to me. "That means you want a *different* kind of drink. Now where were we? Shall we invite Daphne Gunn?"

"Ugh. No. Like over my dead body. Besides she looks like a fucking potato."

She put her pen down. "Simon, that is absolutely intolerable."

"All right, I'm sorry. But no, I hate her. She can't come."

"It would be very classy if you asked her. It would show that you're *above the fray*."

"Well, I'm not."

"Do you ever speak to her?"

"No, never. It's like she's dead."

"Well, it's your party. That's the thing about a party. You invite whomever you want. So we'll put Daphne in the holding tank for the moment."

"I should have those Catholic girls. They're really pretty."

"Oh yes, especially that tall one. She's a stunner, that girl. What's her name?"

"Anna."

"Anna. Yes. What a beauty. Does she have a beau? They always have beaux, those girls."

She sat back and did that thing she always did when she was having a good time, cupping her elbow in her hand and holding her cigarette just to the side of her face. She always did it just before she made some observation. "My God, Simon," she said, "you have such blue eyes it just kills me. *Blueberry* blue.

And so on it went until finally the waiter was hanging around the table and we felt sort of compelled to order something to eat. That's the thing with those French waiters. They can make you feel guilty about anything. They don't have to say a word.

"So when you do want to have your *do*?" she said.

"Can we have it before the old man gets out of the hospital?"

It was like everything just sagged and I instantly had the feeling I'd done something wrong.

"That's mean," she said softly.

"I don't mean it to be mean. It's just more fun when he's not around."

The waiter came by. He took a saucer from the table, spotted a soiled serviette on the floor, picked it up and moved off.

"You're right," I said, "they *have* got radar."

But she didn't answer.

I didn't want to wreck dinner, not with her all dressed up like that and the two of us normally such great company.

"Well *you* shouldn't feel bad," I said.

"Well I do. It makes me feel like I've been a bad parent."

"You've been a great parent."

She was silent.

"I mean it," I said. "When I have kids I'm going to raise them exactly like you did."

She gave me this quick look and I suddenly imagined her as a young girl, tall with big, handsome features.

"Really?" she said. "Do you really think I've done a good job?"

"I really do."

"You're sure?"

"You bet."

She grabbed up her pack of cigarettes and shook one out.

"God, I'm terrible," she said. "I feel like another martini. Would you think I was a terrible old drunk if I had another martini?"

Back home, I went straight up to the maid's room. Well, it's not the maid's room any more. She got canned for butting her cigarettes out in the cat box. But since my Easter report card, I'd been getting sent up there every night to do my homework. It's not a bad little spot really, canary yellow, very away from things. You can hear people coming up the stairs so nobody ever gets the drop on you. Especially my old man, who makes a big racket.

I was supposed to be doing my physics homework but there's something about that textbook, something sinister about the cover that really got to me. Filled me with a kind of dread when I looked at it. I even dreamt about it: it's the night before my final exam and I'm flipping through the book and I suddenly realize that I haven't seen *any* of these pages before, all those diagrams of soup cans with the fucking arrows going every which-way, and I realize that I'm screwed, I'm going to flunk my whole year because in my school, if you fail even one subject, you go back to square one the next fall and all the little squirts who are shorter than you, well suddenly they're sitting beside you in the same grade and all your friends are sitting at a different table for lunch, doing different stuff after school. I mean a complete nightmare, man.

So I pulled out *Scaramouche* and started reading it. This wasn't a complete goof-off, it was on my English course and I'd just gotten to the part where he's invented a new manoeuvre with his sword, I mean I just loved it, but I also knew I was getting way ahead of the class, I'd be finished a month early and then I'd probably flunk the test because I wouldn't be able to remember anything that happened. Sometimes you just can't win.

I heard Harper out in the hallway. He's my brother, two years older than me, the good sheep of the family. Good marks (but not too good), good at sports, the whole business. But not an asshole, not a bully. I gave him a shout.

"Harper," I said, "the old lady thinks I should have a party."
He popped his head in the door.
"Yeah?"
"Yeah."
"What do you think?"
"I don't know. Do you have any friends?"

"A couple."

"Well there you go. Why don't you invite that chick from Bishop Strachan. The one with the big tits. What's her name?"

"Massey. Evelyn Massey."

"I can't believe she's only fifteen."

"Well, she is."

"She reminds me of Marilyn Monroe. That little kid's voice."

"Yeah. Well she doesn't really hang around with our crowd."

"Now there's a girl I'd like to submarine. You ever submarined anybody Simon?" He didn't wait for me to answer. "I love it. I'd like to drink a glass of it."

"Anyway."

"It's not a bad idea," he said, once he got his mind off going down on Evelyn Massey.

"Having a party?"

"Yeah."

"How come?"

"Well you *go* to them all the time, Simon. Might not be a bad idea to have one. That way people won't think you're a big fucking sponge."

"Food for thought," I said, and we both laughed.

"I'm going to watch TV," he said.

"What's on?"

"Fuck all."

"Right."

By the time I was ready for bed, I figured it was a pretty good idea, this party, I figured no sweat. It was even starting to seem like my own idea. I got into my pyjamas and brushed my teeth and looked at my profile about a hundred times in the mirror and then I came back into the bedroom. Plopped my retainer in my mouth. It tasted a bit grungy, it'd been sitting in my drawer since the morning, but I dipped it in a glass of water and it freshened up just fine.

Harper was already in bed, listening to the radio.

"I think I'm going to do it," I said.

"Uh-huh," he said, not giving a shit.

"Maybe I will invite Evelyn Massey." This time he wouldn't bite.

"I got to listen to this." It was a baseball game. I got into bed and flipped open a Beatles book, a glossy one. Harper turned out the light.

"Thanks," I said.

He waited a second.

"Don't mention it."

All of which was cool except that I woke up at four in the morning, my heart jumping around. I was full of the most awful dread. I lay there blinking my eyes, trying to figure out what it was. Then I got it. It was the party. It was like the worst idea in the world, nobody would come, just three ugly chicks and I'd be left standing there, the laughing stock of the school. The party that nobody went to. Honestly, I just couldn't imagine a worse fate. I lay there in the dark thinking what a shitty idea this party was, thinking of how to get out of it without looking totally pathetic. To make things worse, it didn't look as black outside as it did a little while ago. I hate it when it gets light like that, the slow, depressing creep of grey across the sky, everything all dark and cosy and private and then the light steals it away, makes everything normal and flat again. I heard a dog bark at the end of the street, Mr Bluestein taking his mutt out. He did that every morning, five-thirty a.m., rain or shine. That's it, I thought, I'm fucked now. And assuming I was fucked, I fell sound asleep.

Funny thing is, when the alarm rang a few hours later I felt fine, not worried at all, the sun was out, it was a clear spring day. "Man, that was nuts," I thought. So I headed off to school, thinking maybe I'd have the party after all.

By the time I got to the top of our street, I could hear the bell ring across the soccer field. That meant I had five minutes to get to my locker, dump my books in the hallway, and get to prayers. Sure was a bitch to start the day that way, all flustered and out of breath, shirt-tail hanging out of my pants, but you didn't want to be late either because that meant you lined up outside Willie Orr's office, he'd been teaching Latin there ever since they spoke it at the school, where you'd get a detention, no questions asked. I made it into my pew just in time, just as all the kids rose with a crash and the masters began their morning parade down the centre aisle, Fairy Flynn swaying back and forth on the organ. They mounted the platform, the headmaster stepped to the podium, we bowed our heads, I closed my eyes, and we said the Lord's Prayer, some of the guys looking but not me, I was sort of afraid to get caught with my eyes open. We had just started the hymn when I noticed this British kid come skittering down the far aisle. He was holding the change in his pocket to stop it from rattling, sort of biting his lower lip, just to let the masters know he knew he was fucking things up by being so late. He was an English kid with a great accent, he sounded like the Queen. I didn't know his name but we sort of nodded to each other in the halls. Truth is, I got a bit self-conscious around him, he seemed like a movie star, that accent and playing on the first cricket team, even though he was my age. I wondered if maybe I should invite him to the party. At least that'd give me something to talk to him about.

By the time recess rolled around I was starving, and even though I hadn't got around to my physics homework yet, I went over to the tuck shop and bought a chocolate donut and a thing of chocolate milk. Christ it tasted good, it made me sort of weak with pleasure. Then I got to talking to a couple of guys and then the bell rang and I ended up in physics class with nothing done. We had this chrome dome for a teacher, a big barrel-chested guy with a bald head. I threw up my arm and asked a question before he even set his books down. That works sometimes, you bombard the guy so that when he gets around to the homework, he feels like he's already heard enough from you and asks somebody else. So he answers my question but then he says, "Since you're so talkative this morning, Mr Albright, why don't you take us through the first velocity problem."

"Well, it's not quite ready, sir," I said.

"What isn't?"

"That particular section."

"You mean you haven't done your homework."

He's a prick too.

I saw the English guy in the hallway after lunch.

"I'm having a little party," I said. My heart was crashing but I invited him anyway. He was very pleased. Up close he didn't seem so spectacular though. Sort of phoney and forced, like he was copying his dad or something, like he knew it was a number that impressed people in a foreign country and so he was playing it to the hilt.

"Awfully decent of you," he said. "A chap doesn't want to presume."

See what I mean? Like total bullshit, but I was afraid he'd see on my face how I was feeling so the next thing I knew I was laughing like a hyena, throwing my head around like he was saying the funniest stuff I'd ever heard in my life. We must have made some kind of spectacle. When I walked away I felt sort of queasy, like I was made out of tinfoil. Fuck me, I thought, I got to stop doing that.

But it was a great scam, this party thing. Instant power.

Take George Hara, for example. He was in Grade Twelve, a year ahead of me. He played on the hockey team and I'd hated him ever since he said something shitty about my goaltending. (Truth is, pucks scare me.) Anyway, one afternoon last winter I was playing in a pick-up game after school and I was on George's team, the second last guy to get picked, natch, and when one of our guys scored, I zipped around the rink hollering, "We scored! We scored!" George waited till I was in earshot and then he said, "What do you mean *we*?"

See what I mean? A real asshole, but he was bigger than me, and mean in a special way—the expressionless, bony face, the lank hair—he scared me. He seemed like the kind of guy who could punch you in the mouth and not feel bad about it. Anyway, for obvious reasons, I kept a low profile on just how much I loathed him. In other words, I said terrible things *about* him, but never *to* him. With my party, I finally had some leverage. He heard me talking about it on the way to the gym, as a matter of fact I sort of raised my voice as I passed him so he couldn't miss it. He may have been good at hockey, but he lived a hell of a long way from the school and sometimes I saw him staring at me out of the window of his dad's car when I was talking to the girls from Bishop Strachan. Later that afternoon, right after sports, I came blasting out the side door of the school and there was George, waiting in the parking lot for his father to pick him up. He looked sort of forlorn out there, tapping his school bag with his foot, killing time, like a guy who didn't have anything to look forward to, and I felt a sort of wave of sympathy for him.

"Hey George!" I hollered. He stopped kicking his bag and waited for me to get there. He even stuck his hands in his pockets like he was a bit uncomfortable. I went right up to him. "Hey man, do you want to come to my party?"

And guess what he said?

I'm telling you, for awhile there, it was like being mayor of the city.

A few days later, we went to visit the old man in the Clinic. It was set in a pretty enough spot, if you like that sort of thing, about a half-hour outside the city. Me, it always makes me nervous leaving town. I always feel like I might be missing something. Call it a hole in my personality, whatever, I just don't care for all that empty space and nobody around. Harper was supposed to come too but he pooped out at the last minute; said he had cricket practice. Right.

Anyway, this place was a grand old mansion in the country. Even the physical whereabouts seemed subdued, like somebody had told the birds to shut the fuck up, didn't they realize the gravity of the situation, all these rich folks going nuts, trying to kill their wives and drinking antifreeze. Or freaking out about money and hitting the sauce, like my dad.

As usual, Mother went in to see him first. I waited outside in the hall. I was watching this old Cleopatra clanking around the halls in her jewellery and smoking a cigarette in a long black holder. She was pretty friendly actually. Very chatty. Probably a drunk, I figured, and her kids stuck her here because she was just too much to have around. I mean fifteen minutes was fine but I can't imagine having that coming at you in the kitchen at eight o'clock in the morning. I mean that's the thing about crazy people: they've got so much energy, they're always up to something, projects, realignments, that kind of thing. She didn't dawdle either, this one, told me she had to speak to a doctor about something going on in France.

Ten minutes went by; not a sound from my dad's room, not a peep, I didn't know what they were doing in there but I started to get self-conscious, the nurses looking at me as they went by. So I went wandering around the halls. There was lots of sunlight streaming in, canned music, all very *up*. But when I turned the corner, I heard a groan coming from behind a door, a really awful, end-of-the-world groan, like only a crazy person who didn't care what anybody thought of them would make. It was so raw, like watching an animal being born and it scared the bejesus out of me. I hurried back to my dad's room. I didn't wait, nothing, I just burst in the door.

My mother was sitting on the bed, holding his hand, and I heard him say, "I just don't have the confidence any more." Then he saw me standing there and this expression of impatience and irritation came over his face. He just closed right up.

"Just a minute," he said, like I was a moron, like I'd turned up at a wedding with jam and cat hair all over my face. "Your mother will be right there."

I went back out into the hall, considerably offended. When I get pissed off like that, I get this sensation in my body, a sort of metallic hollowness, and I can't get rid of it unless I complain about it to the person who made me feel like that. But with my dad—he was from the old school, in case I haven't mentioned it—he didn't figure it was my place to talk back. So you never really got to have it out with him. It just left you sick with rage and planning to stick him with a pitchfork.

I glared at a nurse who looked at me. Even my posture

changed. I leaned against the wall and crossed my arms. It felt sort of familiar. Then I remembered why. It was the way I stood in the hall when I got kicked out of class for being an asshole. Same exact way.

"Oh yeah, *that's* what he's like," I thought to myself. "For a second there, I thought I actually missed him."

A few minutes later my mother fluttered out, all anxious and smiley and trying to make everything all right.

"He's not feeling well," she said. I snorted. I shouldn't have but I did. It was partly to punish her for not taking my side, for not getting it. I went right in.

My father was lying in bed in blue pyjamas. His face was grey, his hands folded across his chest like a stiff. Naturally he said nothing about kicking me out a moment earlier. 'Sorry' would have done the trick, I would have melted with surprise; I would have melted with gratitude, too, because it would have freed me from feeling like I had a belt around my chest.

He asked me about school, about a test I'd knocked out of the park the week before, math no less.

"There was this isosceles triangle problem but there was a mistake in it. Like in the typing. So instead of solving it, I proved that you *couldn't* solve it."

"Uh-huh," he said. "That's good. That's very good."

He wasn't listening to a fucking word I said, a dummy could see that, and I got instantly pissed off at myself for letting him play me like a sucker again, me coming up there thinking he'd be glad to see me and all. But no, he was just putting up with me, as usual.

"It's been nice to see you," I said.

We shook hands. I went back out into the hall. My mother was out there, smoking a cigarette.

"How'd it go?" she asked.

I laughed.

"Don't be like that," she snapped. "It's so unattractive."

I waited a couple of beats. I could feel my face distorting. Like the muscles were moving it as if they had a mind of their own.

"Yeah, well don't feel compelled to bring me next time," I said.

I called up a whole mess of people that night. Part of me was ready for them to say, "A party? At your place? Now why the *fuck* would I go to a party at your place?" But it didn't go like that, not at all. My mother was right. People like being invited places, even by an asshole, not that I was one, but if they've got a choice, they'd rather not go than not be invited. It sort of gained momentum, this ringing people up, and by the end I was really speedy, like it was a race or something. I had so much juice I even called up a few people I hadn't intended to invite. What the hell, I thought, it's a party, but really it was just an excuse to *keep at it.* I kept making the same joke over and over, like it just occurred to me.

"Hi Leonard," I'd say, "not that I expect anybody to come, but I'm having a little party," and then I'd laugh like I'd never said it before. Which was fine until I accidentally called him back.

"You already said that," he said.

Most guys would have let it go but not Leonard. He was a little bit *exact* for my comfort.

I saved the girls for the end. I called up Susan Fairley first, she had a fierce crush on me, a one-way crush I might add, but I knew she'd come. I called Adrienne Mustard, the doctor's daughter, and told her to bring Mary-Anne Parker. Then the Bishop Strachan girls, Jane Martin and Rodent and Jamie Porter, who would let you do a lot if you could just get her alone. And that went so well, I started to call the tougher cases, those pretty Catholic girls, Pamela Mathews and Anna Christie and Cynthia Macdonald, who was so beautiful she scared me. Somebody asked me if they should tell Daphne Gunn and I said sure, why not.

On the night of the party, Friday, I came home right after school. My mother had done everything, natch. She was whirling around the house like it was *her* party.

"I've got the potato chips, pretzels, Coke, orange pop, dip, I know you don't like it but some kids do."

"What are the green things?" I asked.

"Don't be negative. They're pickles. You don't have to eat them."

"I can smell them from here."

"Then go stand somewhere else. Gosh, I forgot the party hats."

My face nearly fell off.

"I'm kidding," she said softly, like it offended her I could even think that.

"You better relax, Simon," my brother said. "This is supposed to be a party."

I went upstairs and left her to it. I took a shower, dried my hair under her hairnet, something that made it just right. Sort of puffy but in a natural way. I mean no one was going to mistake me for Troy Donahue but I knew that going in. I put on a pair of crisp black slacks, a shirt and a blue sweater. Brought out my eyes, my mother always said. I put on the old man's deodorant,

Old Spice, but I already had my shirt on, so I had to undo a couple of buttons and squeeze it in there. I was worried about wrecking my hair by moving around too much. I brushed my teeth, gargled till I gagged.

"Jesus, Simon," Harper said through the bathroom door, "What the fuck's going on in there?"

I heard my mother yell from downstairs where she was not minding her own business.

"Harper. Language."

"Oh yeah," he said over the balcony, "like he's never heard those words before."

"That's not the point," she said. Not mad or anything. Just sure.

He let it go, which was good because he had about one more smart-ass remark left before she got pissed off.

A couple of pals turned up before the official beginning. They were all dressed up, you could smell them, soap and deodorant and shampoo. We were all pretty excited and being around each other, what with a whole party ahead of us, it was intoxicating. But right through this, like out of nowhere, I had the weirdest thought, the kind that makes you think you belong in a booby hatch. I imagined my mother walking into my bedroom, all drained of colour, and saying, "Something terrible has happened to your father, you have to cancel the party."

I dream this shit up just to torture myself. Sometimes I think it's because I've got bad, black flecks in my blood and every so often they pass through my brain. I read a story once about a guy whose wife was having a baby. He was right there in the delivery room with her, and all he could think of was the Nazis throwing babies into ovens. And I remember thinking, that's fucked up, boy, that's really fucked up. There's a million other things that guy ought to be thinking about. So there I was, the party's just starting and I'm thinking about Nazis and babies and my dad dying. Fortunately some more people turned up at the door.

My mother disappeared like she'd promised and left me with the whole downstairs.

Around nine-thirty I looked around and I realized that even if nobody else came, I was still home free. There must have been a vacuum that Friday night, and everybody decided to do one thing, like those lemmings all deciding every ten years or so to throw themselves off a cliff. People hung around in the kitchen, in the living room, even in the foyer. They went to the fridge, they took stuff, they acted like they'd been there a hundred times before. It was great. In fact, I had to flush a couple of them out of the basement. They were getting ready for something serious down there.

There was this guy from New York, he was a boarder at school. Usually those guys are all queers, everybody knows that, but this guy was sort of cool, he had wonderful shirts, pink ones and yellow ones, he wore them under his school blazer. Come to think of it, he looked like one of those guys who reads *Playboy*, you know, *What kind of man reads* Playboy? He had that kind of sophistication. He asked me if I'd let him play the records. It'd give him something to do besides sitting on the couch, looking like a goof. Course he got to meet everybody that way, everybody being an expert on what you should play at a party.

Dorian Bradshaw and some of the guys from the Catholic school hung around in the driveway, leaning against the old man's car and drinking. Just as long as they didn't get into a fight, I didn't care. Some of those guys, I'll tell you, they can go berserko. One of them grabbed a spray can once at a party and wrote his name on the bedroom wall. Like in a complete stranger's house. It wasn't real hard to figure out who did it. Anyway, I didn't want any of that shit at my party, so when they came back in, reeking, I kept an eye on them.

Harper mostly stayed up in his room. He had kind of an outbreak with his skin, it wasn't his fault, I mean he didn't eat chocolate or anything but it made him a little shy. One time he came down and made toast. I asked him if he wanted to hang around.

"No," he said. "Thanks anyway. Not really my scene."

She was wearing a blue, sparkly dress with little cotton straps on her shoulders. And a lot of eye make-up. From a certain angle, she looked sort of Asian. I heard her tell somebody this famous folk singer had written a song for her. I figured that was bullshit but there was enough to her you couldn't be completely sure. I mean if you saw her in a Hollywood restaurant, you'd probably really envy her.

Pretty full of herself. Kept throwing these quick little looks around the room to see who was watching her. She came with a guy named Mitch. I didn't invite him, he's just one of those guys figures he's welcome everywhere. And he usually is. Cowboy good looks, pale blue eyes (like a Siberian husky) and white teeth, quite a hit with the girls, on first impression anyway. He caught me staring at her. I dropped my glance too late. I didn't want him to think I was a loser, pining after somebody else's date.

I drifted around the living room to see how the party was doing. I ran into Daphne Gunn. She was the one who dropped me for playing spin the bottle with her best friend while she was in the hospital with a broken leg. That's what she said anyway. I knew it was bullshit. She just liked somebody else better, this guy, Danny Lang. In fact she probably put her friend up to it. Weird how much I missed her once she was gone. I walked around like a sick dog for a couple of days, maybe even a week. I even burst into tears one day in my mother's bathroom because it occurred to me, just like that, out of the blue, that I couldn't ride my bike over to Daphne's house any more. I mean that's what was so haunting about it, this thing that I used to do all the time I couldn't do any more.

Anyway. She came with her new boyfriend, a guy with a funny-shaped head. To be fair he wasn't a goof. Just sort of extraneous.

"Who's Mr Cylinder Head?" I asked.

"He's my new boyfriend."

"Son of a gun," I said, meaning I'm not sure what.

She introduced him. I didn't want him feeling superior or anything, just because he had her and I didn't, so I played my cards very carefully. I waited till I'd said something especially funny and then I split. I've got an exquisite sense of timing. I really know how to do that stuff.

There was a ton of people by now. I saw George Hara smoking a cigarette by the fireplace. He was wearing a cardigan with a shirt under it buttoned up at the collar. Very square. I guess he really *didn't* go out very much. Nobody dressed like that in my part of town. The English guy didn't come, which was all right because I'd have had to pay a lot of attention to him on account of him not knowing anybody. But I don't know. I always feel responsible for everybody having a good time. It's probably bullshit. I mean according to me it's amazing they get their shoes tied without me around.

Four girls sat on the floor, their kilts pushed between their knees. They asked me to sit with them but I was too restless. I'd chat a bit here and there but then I'd move on. I had the damnedest sensation of looking for something, of waiting for something to happen. So I'd get to the end of the room and then I'd turn around and go through the whole works again.

I went upstairs. I heard my mother talking to a couple of kids just outside the bathroom. But she was doing a good job so I left them alone. It's a great ace up your sleeve, having a mother people like. It makes you look better. Then I remembered the couple in the basement, I wondered if they'd snuck back there.

I went downstairs. I opened the basement door and you'll never guess what I saw. I saw the girl in the sparkly dress; only she wasn't with Mitch, she was with some other guy, a prefect at my school, she had her head turned up and she was kissing him on the mouth, I could see her lower jaw moving. They broke apart when they saw me. I went back upstairs sort of shocked.

In a little while she came into the kitchen. I could feel her looking at me as she worked her way across the room. I opened the refrigerator and pretended to peer in. Then she was standing beside me. I could smell her.

"You remind me of somebody," she said.

"Oh yes?"

"What does your father do?"

"He's a stockbroker."

"That sounds pretty interesting."

I looked at her blankly.

Somebody spilled a drink on the floor. I frowned.

"Don't worry," she said, "Somebody'll clean it up."

"Are you a model or something?" I asked.

"Only in the summer. The rest of the time I'm just like you."

I doubt that, I thought.

"That's a nice haircut." I said. "What does *your* dad do?"

"My father works in the movies," she said.

"Oh yeah?"

"He knows everybody."

"Does he know Kenny Withers?"

"Probably. Who's Kenny Withers?"

"He's a friend of mine. He lives down the street. He collects stamps."

She looked at me coolly.

"That's very funny." She waited a moment. "Do you have a girlfriend?"

"No." I was sorry as soon as I said it.

"I'll bet you do. I'll bet she's just not here tonight. I'll bet you're a two-timer."

"What's your name?" I asked.

"Scarlet Duke."

"Is that your real name?"

"You want to see some ID?" She reached around to a cloth purse that hung from her bare shoulder.

"No, no."

"Here," she said. "Smell that." She put a wrist under my nose. I could see a little blue vein.

"It's Boucheron. Very expensive." She looked at me. "Nice eh?"

"Yes, very nice."

"$110 a bottle."

"How did you get here, Scarlet?"

"The guy I came with is a friend of the guy who lives here."

"Your boyfriend?"

"He's not really my boyfriend."

"*I* live here."

She looked startled. Very cool to have so much effect on her. "You live here?"

"Yes."

"By yourself?"

"No, with my mother. And my father. I got a brother too."

Mitch came over. His blond hair that fell just so over his forehead.

"Cool party," he said.

Scarlet looked at a small gold watch on her wrist. "I have to go. My father will have a bird." She extended her hand. "Nice to meet you." I could smell her perfume again. "Think about me sometime," she said. And then they left.

I cleaned up the spilt drink. Somebody got loose in the pantry and opened a can of corn. Spilled it too. Somebody turned on the TV but I unplugged it. You can't have a TV on at a party. Rosemary Shank was sick in the bathroom. She always did that, got drunk and got a guy to look after her. But really, the party was a hit, little clusters of people sitting on the floor, the lights off, a candle here and there, everybody talking. I wondered why I'd never had one before.

And that girl. After the party was over, I sat for a little while in the living room. It was sort of like a battlefield the day after: half-empty glasses of coke, one with a cigarette butt in it, coagulated pieces of pizza, which tasted pretty good. Records out of their covers, a cushion squashed down on the chesterfield. And then that girl. I saw her chin moving when she kissed that guy; they must have been really going at it. The skin all soft under her chin. She was really something.

CHAPTER TWO

BECAUSE WE WERE RICH LITTLE PRICKS we got out of
school for the summer three weeks before everybody
else. But first we had exams. My brother was writing the
provincial finals, which was a big deal, him walking around
the upstairs hallway with *King Lear* in his hand (it had a purple
cover), looking out the window and whispering to himself. His
skin had broken out again. He was mighty uptight. So was I, to
be honest.

I got through History all right, I aced English, Latin was a
breeze, I passed Math, maybe a 60, but then there was the last
one, Physics. Sure enough, just like I'd predestined it, the night
before my exam I open that book with the scary cover, I'm
looking at the soup cans and I've never seen them before. I study
till around midnight, till I've got sand in my eyes and then I go
to bed up in the maid's room. I set the alarm for four o'clock. I
check it about five times. I turn out the light. I close my eyes. I
sink right down to the bottom of the tank. I mean I'm like a dead
man, lying there on the bottom, when the alarm goes off. I think
it can't be four o'clock, not yet, I've just got to sleep, there must
be something wrong with the clock. So I pick it up in the dark
and I squint at it. Fuck me: Four it is. I'm so tired I feel sick to my
stomach, like something really bad is going to happen if I don't

go right back to sleep. I feel like calling for my mother and getting her to write me a note, saying I can't come to school today. Simon's not feeling well. You can say that again.

But I get up and go over and sit at the desk, staring at the yellow wall, wrapped in a blanket. I open the horrible physics book. I turn the pages: more soup cans, more arrows.

After awhile I can hear the city waking up, I hear Bluestein's mutt, I hear a car drive down the street, a solitary car, the first of the day. It's sort of a relief actually when the sunlight comes through the window, it means I'm getting near the end. I go down to the kitchen and get some orange juice and toast and come back up to the maid's room.

It's an afternoon exam so I leave the house around noon. The street has a strange feel to it, and I realize it's because I never come along here at this time. But it's a pretty spring day, the sun high up in the sky; the clouds are long and feathery and the air smells sweet. I get to school an hour early. Some of the guys like to hang around the exam room, yacking like crazy, asking each other questions, but I don't do that. I figure somebody'll ask me something I don't know and it'll rattle the shit out of me. So I stay away. I feel like I'm balancing a big medicine ball on top of my head and any sudden movement in any direction will make it fall off and I won't remember a thing. I head out to the soccer field. There's nobody there and I settle down in the grass, me and my physics book. I lie on my stomach. I can see the school from here, I can see the boys, little tiny figures milling around the front door, I can hear their voices coming across the grounds. I can smell the grass. I look down and I can see an ant crawling around. I part the grass carefully and I watch him.

I finally open up the physics book. The sun reflects off the pages, it makes me squint, I stare down at the book, I start to read but after awhile I realize I'm thinking about being in the boat up at our cottage, I'm thinking of the chink-chink the waves make under the hull on a choppy day. I turn the page, I look at it, but my attention just slides off like an egg slipping off a plate. Same for the next page. I can't read any more, I can't read another word or think about anything more and if it's on the exam, well, that's too bad for me. So I close the book, I just stretch out, I put my hand under my chin and I just wait there in the warm grass.

The exam went all right. I mean it didn't make me sign up for science camp or anything, but I didn't bomb out either. Funny thing about that book, though. The textbook. Like the minute I got out of the exam, it went from being the most important book in the world, right in the centre of the universe, to just a pile of pages with doodles all over them. It even *looked* different. I brought it home though. I was too superstitious to leave it lying around on a windowsill at school. I was afraid it might get pissed off at me and arrange things so I flunked. You can never be too careful.

Next day, we packed up the car and headed north to our cottage. The old man stayed in the Clinic. Which was just fine with me.

It was about a three-hour drive to get there and we always stopped at the same place for something to eat. It was a little roadside joint with fabulous hamburgers. Some local guy ran it but he turned it into a big deal, every summer it got bigger, more kids working on the grill, pretty girls taking your order in the parking lot.

"How come we never go anywhere else?" I said as I burst out of the car. It wasn't really a question, I was just happy to be out of school and I wanted to talk. But Harper was a little grumpy that day.

"I don't know," he grunted, "good burgers, I guess." There was no point asking what was bugging him, he'd just tell you to buzz off. He wasn't like me that way. I can't keep anything to myself. I mean I find it physically difficult to keep my mouth shut.

Anyway. Out in the parking lot, the old lady opened a thermos of vodka and orange juice, she'd whipped it up before she left home, and poured herself a drink. She opened the car door and left it open. She had this crazy idea that you could drink in your car as long as you had one foot on the ground. She kept the car door open so she could get her leg out extra fast in case a cop walked by. Jesus. What these folks wouldn't do for a noggin. Like I mean, what with the old man getting soused in the living room, night after night, you'd think this wasn't such a hot idea. Everybody walking around in a fucking blur. Getting pissed off at stuff they couldn't even remember in the morning. One night when I was little, like in grade seven, he called me downstairs to look at my math homework. Talk about looking for trouble. Course it was all screwed up, mistakes all over the place and next thing I know is he hurls the notebook into the air, it's flapping there like some kind of bird and I'm running for cover.

I sort of daydreamed that he'd stay in the Clinic all summer, which I know is a bad thing to admit, but at least nobody'd have to be nervous around him. No more walking around like you're in a minefield, wondering what's going to set him off, a wet towel on the bed, borrowing a comb and not putting it back. I mean get this, one morning I get up for school, I'm twelve years old and I can't find my comb. So I go into his bedroom and I pick up his off the night table and I wander around the house, combing my hair, looking here and there, in this mirror, that mirror, I don't know, I'm twelve remember, and next thing I know he comes charging into my bedroom, fit to be tied, and he wants to know where his comb is. So I say I don't know. He asks me if I borrowed it and stupidly I tell him the truth, I say, yeah I did. Well that just sets him off. He just about has a fucking stroke right there in his business suit. I can smell the Old Spice when he comes close to me. I can also feel my behind contracting violently.

"The next time you take my comb," he says, just shaking, "I'm going to give you a beating!"

And the thing is, he meant it. He really did.

Anyway. Enough about him.

Point is, after awhile, you wish people like that would just stay away.

Anyway, we're driving north. We get to Huntsville, we go through town real slow, I'm looking this way, that way, for my summer pals, Greg with the bad teeth, and his sexy sister. I see Mr Jewel who owns the shoe store; Chip Peterson who's good at golf; we go by the hardware store and cross over the bridge, it rings like a big hollow drum under the car, there's Blackburn's Marina where we gas up the boat, Loblaw's, the Tastee Queen where we go after the dance at Teen Town. It's all there, just the same as last summer. I see Sandy Hunter on the side of the road, she must be coming home from school, her hair all long and blonde. We pick up speed. Seven point three miles to go. I know all the houses, the barns, the hilltops from here on in. I undo the window and I can feel the air blow on my face. Smells completely different than it does in the city.

We turn off the road and go down the lane. Trees on both sides, you can hear the branches scrape the side of the car. You can hear our little stream, which runs through the ravine. There's our mailbox, all rusted from the winter. Pebbles crunching under the car wheels. We come around a corner and there it is, a big field and our house at the far end. Rambling, a white clapboard house with a double garage and green shutters. There's my room, top right-hand side, overlooking the garage. I'm so impatient to get going I can hardly breathe. I get out of the car. I want to do everything in my summer vacation all in the next hour. But I have to help bring the stuff into the house, groceries and suitcases and pillow slips stuffed with fresh bedding, all kinds of stuff, records, even a plant. Then I run upstairs to my room. I love the way it smells, all unused and empty, there's a sort of exciting mothbally tang. The cowboys on the wallpaper from when I was a little squirt, the old clothes in the drawer that don't fit me any more, a skindiving magazine, an old *Field and Stream*. A book on graphology. I flip it open. All my notes in the margin. Jesus, remember that? Man, I really worked at it. Last chapter is called "How to Recognize a Murderer."

From my window I can see all the way down to the lake. All the leaves aren't grown in. It's not really summer up here yet. The water is too cold for swimming; it's sort of colourless and foreign this time of year. But it's going to warm up just fine and in a month it'll be like soup. That's what my mother always says when she slips off the dock into the water, a towel around her head. "My God, boys," she says, "it's like soup."

And then I set off, I zip all over the house, into the bathroom, the empty bedroom at the end of the hall, the old man's room, I check the cupboards in the downstairs hallway, I love the way they smell, too. Then I go into the basement. That's where I set up my drums. Well I don't have a set of drums, they're too noisy I'm told, so I set up a whole lot of books, just like a drum kit. Plus I've got an old cymbal with a chunk missing, a plastic garbage can lid for a high hat and an old record player. I mounted the whole works on a platform, to give it a sense of occasion, as they say. Man, the daydreams I've had down there. I won't even go into it. But you know what I mean.

Cha-la-la-la-la,
It's not the way you smile
That breaks my heart
Cha-la-la-la-la.

There's all sorts of old stuff down there, pots covered in spider webs, old photograph albums, a bait box, a workbench, a wonky ping-pong table. Sometimes I feel sort of sorry for the basement, it's like a person nobody ever visits. I feel like I'm its only protector, the only one in the house that shows any interest in it. If it weren't for me nobody would care for that place at all. But it also spooks me sometimes, particularly at night. There's a light bulb down there that you have to turn off before you can go up the stairs. You've got to do that last little bit completely in the dark. And sometimes when I'm about half up the stairs, I can feel the hair rise on the back of my neck, I have a feeling that somebody is going to come out from behind the furnace and grab me by the ankles. I don't know how many times I've come blasting into the kitchen like I've been shot out of a cannon.

Anyway, I'm down there for awhile, fooling around, when I hear Harper at the top of the stairs.

"Let's go down to the dock," he says, which means that his bad mood has lifted. And I say sure and we head out.

Must have been a couple of weeks later. I was in my mother's bedroom one afternoon, listening to a Latin zither record. She went to town once a week and cleaned out the local record store, I mean she bought everything, Pete Fountain and his clarinet, Elvis Presley's Golden Hits, Dave Brubeck, soundtracks from Italian movies, the works. It was corny stuff, this Latin zither, but romantic and it made me sentimental, sad about stuff that had never even happened. My mother had this great big picture window in her bedroom, it was huge, you could spread out your arms and not even touch the sides. You could see everything, the field going down to the marsh, the lake all blue and sparkly, a country road way, way off in the distance, and sometimes when the sun was setting, there was a gold light that covered everything. You couldn't believe anything could be so pretty.

I heard the phone ring at the other end of the house. It rang a couple of times and then it stopped. I waited. I heard footsteps coming toward me.

"Simon, it's for you."

I figured it was Greg, the guy with the bad teeth. We were going to Teen Town that night. He looked okay in there, you could hardly notice his teeth. I picked up the phone.

"Do you remember me?" It was a sort of boyish voice but it was a girl.

"Scarlet?"

"Boy, you got a good memory."

"I recognized your voice."

"A lot of people do. I got your number from a friend of yours."

"Oh yeah?"

"A guy at your party."

"Who was it?"

"I can't remember his name. Not really my type. I hope you don't mind me calling you."

"No, not at all."

"I mean there's not very much you could say about it, is there?"

There was a pause.

"Listen, do you remember that guy I was with?" she said.

"Mitch? "

"Yeah."

"He dumped me."

"Really?"

"Yeah."

"Well, he never really struck me as your type. If you know what I mean." I sort of jumped into this sentence without thinking about it, and now I was stuck inside it.

"No, I don't."

"Well, he just didn't seem like the kind of person you are."

"What kind of person is that?"

"Sort of . . ." I waited for the word to come, "complicated."

"You're complicated, too," she said. "I could tell."

"Oh yeah? How?"

"Just by the stuff you said. Not having a girlfriend and not caring if anybody knew."

"Well, I've had a girlfriend before."

"Yeah, but it doesn't mean anything, just *having* one. Just for the sake of it."

"Exactly. You don't want to brag or anything."

That stumped her.

"What do you mean?"

"Well, there are some things you don't want to get caught doing and tooting your own horn is definitely one of them."

"What are the other things?"

"What?"

"The other things you don't want to get caught doing?"

"Well, never mind about that."

"Tell me."

"We don't really know each other well enough to get into that stuff."

"So you've had a girlfriend before?"

"A couple."

"Do you have one now?"

"Not at this very moment."

"Yeah, but is there somebody out there thinking they're your girlfriend?"

"Not unless they're mentally ill."

"Listen," she said, "when are you coming back down to the city?"

I went outside looking for Harper. He was driving golf balls into the ravine.

"Don't you think the old man is going to notice he's missing a few balls?"

"Nah," he said. "He won't notice fuck-all."

Harper brought down the club and whacked one into the blue sky; it hung there for a moment and then crackled as it fell through the trees.

"That's a beauty," I said. He teed up another ball.

"This chick just called me."

"Oh yeah?"

"The chick from my party."

"It wasn't Evelyn Massey, was it?"

"No, she didn't come, remember? It was somebody else."

"God, I'd really like to go down on her."

"Yeah, you told me. No, this was somebody else. You remember that chick in the sparkly dress."

"The good-looking one?"

"Scarlet."

"That her name?"

"Yep."

"That's a fucked-up name."

"Anyway."

For an older brother, Harper was sort of weirdly sensitive, and he could see I'd come out there to talk to him about the girl.

"So she called you?" he said.

"Yeah. Out of the blue."

"What'd she want?"

"She just broke up with her boyfriend."

"Really?"

"Who broke up with who?"

I hesitated a second.

"It was kind of mutual."

"That's a good one."

"What do you mean?"

"If he broke up with her and she's on the blower in two seconds to another guy, you don't have to be a fucking genius to figure that one out."

"Like she's getting even?"

"Or making him jealous or some such bullshit."

"You figure?"

"People fall in love, they break up, they do all sorts of shitty things to each other. Remember that cunt Judy Strickland."

I didn't want to talk about Judy Strickland just now.

"She was a cunt, that girl. Somebody should've taken her out behind the woodshed and put her down. Right at birth."

"Anyway, Scarlet wanted to know when I was coming down to the city."

"Yeah, well don't bet the farm on it."

He teed up another ball.

"Judy Strickland. Proof positive that all human beings are *not* created equal," he said and whacked a ball into the valley.

"You can tell by the click," he said. "When the club makes that kind of a click, you know it's a beauty."

Just then the side door opened and the old lady came out through the garage. She had her shirt tied at her waist, like Harry Belafonte. She must have seen us gabbing from the kitchen window and she wanted to know what was cooking. I started to tell her. Harper went inside right in the middle of it, he'd already heard the story and I was sort of sorry to see him go, it was like it wasn't interesting enough to hear a second time but once he was gone for awhile I was glad because I didn't have to be hip about how I described it to my mother.

A couple of days later, she went off to visit Aunt Marnie in Algonquin Park. They were old pals from high school. Must have been sometime in the '30s. Long time ago, anyway. Aunt Marnie wasn't really my aunt, I just called her that; she was sort of a dumpy woman with funny black glasses and this wild cackle. She used to make my mother laugh so hard she'd like fear for her safety, all bent over in the kitchen, red face, begging Aunt Marnie to lay off, she was killing her. Like I remember once them going on about Bobodiolous, this city somewhere in Africa, the two of them in the kitchen just crippled about it. "I think I might stop off in Bobodiolous for a week or two," my mother would say. Or, "I don't know. That sounds like a Bobo-diolousian accent to me," and then they'd like collapse, both of them, and it would just start up, that wild cackle, just the sound of it making my mother laugh even harder. God, they were demento those women, when they got together. Just demento.

Anyway, she went off to see Aunt Marnie and she left Harper and me in charge of the house.

"Don't burn the place to the ground," she said and got in her big grey Pontiac and we watched it bomb up the driveway, a big cloud of dust rising up behind it and then she whizzed around the corner and she was gone.

That night Harper and me were going to a dance over at Hidden Valley. They were the best dances around and people used to come all the way from Barrie and Bracebridge and Parry Sound, all these kids coming to this one chalet for the dance. They brought in big bands, some from Toronto, but sometimes as far away as England. I saw the Hollies there once. They did that song, "Bus Stop." Very weird to hear it like that, not on the radio, but right there in front of you.

The dance was right across the bay so we took the boat. We cut the engine halfway across and just drifted. It was so quiet out there in the lake, the water black, just like ink. Nothing moving.

"Put your hand in," Harper said. "It's like soup."

"We should go swimming."

"I just got my hair right," he said.

"Right. Me too."

"It'll wash all the deodorant off."

"You need it in that place."

We were silent for awhile, the boat just hanging there in space. Across the water you could hear a girl's voice; then a screen door slammed.

"God, it's eerie how you can hear everything." We listened for a few moments.

"I wish I had a girl here," Harper said. "I might try to take Annie Kincaid home in the boat tonight. Can you get a ride if I do?"

"Who would I get a ride from?"

"Just do me a favour, will you, if I give you the signal? Don't come up and ask me when we're going home."

"Hardly," I said.

"And don't tell the old lady."

"I won't."

A boat puttered by us, its bow light all green and holy.

"I'm looking forward to Christmas," I said,

"Christmas?" he said, "Where the fuck did that come from? Was it that light on the bow?"

"Yeah," I said, "I like it when it's all cold and snowy. I sort of miss it."

"What time is it?" Harper asked after awhile.

"Time you got a watch."

"No, really, we don't want to get there too early. Look like a pair of fucking losers."

"We should dress like twins. You know, matching cardigans."

"Right. A pair of *real* assholes."

I heard him laugh in the dark.

"Never could figure out why those guys do that. Dress the same. Even when they're grown up. It's completely fucked up."

"Exactly."

"So what time is it?"

"It's ten o'clock."

"Better sit out here a bit longer."

He spread himself out on the seat, putting his feet up on the side of the boat. Arms behind his head. I lay back on the other seat and the two of us just floated out onto the black lake, staring up at the stars and saying fuck-all.

I saw Sandy Hunter in the line-up but I pretended not to see her. She was a local girl, went to high school up here. I met her at a dance last summer where she was wearing this white shirt (you could see she had real tits underneath, the way the shirt was pushed out), and when Greg introduced me to her, I was so nervous I could hardly talk. I don't think I even looked at her. Anyway, must have been a few nights later, I looked up her number in the phone book and with my heart thumping like a fucking rabbit, I gave her a call. I even made a list of stuff to talk about, so I didn't run out. Anyway, it went all right. But it was the damndest thing, soon as she started to like me, she stopped seeming so good-looking. I grew distinctly cool toward her and then one day when one of her friends told me that she told her that I'd kissed her, I pretended it was big betrayal, you know, the sort of thing she shouldn't have told anybody about and I used it as an excuse to dump her. She called me up a few times after that, sort of bawling, which made me like her even less, but I felt guilty, like somebody who's run over a dog: you just want to back up the car and finish them off.

Finally she cooled it and stopped calling me, the rest of the summer went by. I didn't get another girlfriend and one night I saw Sandy again at the Teen Town dance. She was wearing a black turtleneck sweater, with those little tits standing out, and I was pretty cocky and confident, I mean I was pretty sure she liked me more than the guy she was with, she was just with him because she couldn't be with me, and this song came on, "Sherry," it was, and I clapped my hands together and I hollered something like, "I just love this song," and then I started to dance, sort of, and she gave me this real cold look, I mean not in the spirit of things at all, and said, "You're so obnoxious."

It went right through me. I felt as if somebody had caught me singing to the mirror or something, I mean I felt like a complete asshole. So ever since then I've sort of stayed away from Sandy Hunter because it's no fun to be around somebody who used to like you a lot and doesn't any more.

I just about had a bird waiting in the line-up to get into the dance. It took like forever. The guy at the door was a disc jockey at the Huntsville radio station, and he was carrying on like a big fucking celebrity and making everybody wait while he flirted with all the chicks. You could hear the band start up and that just made me homicidal with impatience.

"Take it easy," Harper said. But I couldn't, I kept sticking my head over the top of the crowd like a giraffe, giving the guy dirty looks. Finally I got to the door.

"About time," I said, but the guy just ignored me. He was talking about his wife, telling some kid he should've waited to get married. Too much temptation. "Sure you look," he said, "it's natural." Like I give a shit, right?

I tore myself away from these two Einsteins and went in. I got a stamp on my hand that glowed when you put it under a purple lamp. Whenever I saw that neon purple at the door to a dance it made me feel like I was entering an exotic kingdom.

I went over and stood by the band. They were a Toronto group, Tommy Graham and the Big Town Boys. I'd seen them on TV a lot, and they seemed kind of corny to me, in their matching striped shirts and white jeans, all of them exactly the same, the kind of rock band that grownups tap their foot out of time to. But I'll tell you, in person they were something else. I mean they could really play, even Tommy who'd always seemed like a bit of a gearbox to me, mincing around with his little white guitar and skinny legs. I used to think to myself, boy, only in Canada would a bunch of gearboxes like these guys get on the air. I mean in England they got the Beatles and the Stones and in the States they got Bob Dylan but up here we get Tommy Graham and the Big Town Boys. But they had a great drummer. He had a set of black Rogers drums, a double tom and a double bass. That's a lot of artillery. I stood by the side of the stage watching him play and I felt just the worst kind of envy. I mean I would have died to do something like that, but he was older than I was, maybe four, five years, so I figured I still had time.

I looked around the room. I didn't want to move or somebody would take my place. I saw Sandy Hunter; she was talking to a tall, sportsy-looking guy with a brushcut. Terry somebody. I think he was captain of the lacrosse team, a real bonehead but you don't want to fool around with a guy like that. He kept giving me looks so I figured she was talking about me, telling him what an asshole I was and he was just dying for the chance for me to do something stupid so he could take me outside into the parking lot and kick the shit out of me. So I made sure I didn't catch his eye.

Greg came up to me but he was pissed. He did that all the time at dances, I mean you'd figure with those teeth he might behave himself, but forget it. Him and a couple of guys had gone drinking in the truck before the dance and he was all big and blustery in a way that made me nervous. Grabbing people and hugging them and all that shit. It was kind of a look-at-how-drunk-I-am number, real noisy, and frankly I didn't want anybody to think he was a friend of mine. Nice eh? Well, there you go. I guess if you're going to get drunk and behave like an asshole, you got to expect people to duck you.

I saw those two sisters from Quebec. Man, they were good-looking, one with light hair, one with black hair; sharp little chins and black eyes. Like a pair of dolls. Sex dolls. They were out of my league, I knew that, I mean there was no point in even trying, although one of them, I have to say, smiled at me sometimes. I think she either felt sorry for me or she thought I was real interesting because I never talked to her. Who knows? Maybe she was just nice. I turned back to watch the band. He could do some pretty fancy footwork, that drummer, he knew I was watching him and every so often he'd look over and give me a nod. With these little round sunglasses and cowboy boots, he was just about the coolest looking guy you've ever seen. I mean he had it all. But I didn't want him to think he had to perform for me all night long, so after awhile I moved across the floor and went upstairs.

From up there I could watch the girls dancing. There's nothing like a girl who can really dance. It's like watching God. Up there you could watch and watch and watch and nobody knew you were staring, or what you were thinking about. The smell of those dancing bodies floated up through the heat and the smoke and the coloured lights. I wondered what those girls did with their sweaty shirts and underwear when they got home. Did they leave them all lying on the bed, did they hang them up in the washroom? I sort of wished I could take their sweaty clothes home, just have them to myself in my bedroom for a little bit. Just thinking like that gave me the most awful kind of plunging sensation. I had to step back and take a deep breath. Otherwise I'd have gone over the balcony.

I saw one of the French Canadian girls, the dark-haired one, standing by the railing and I gave her a sort of formal hello. And when she didn't call the cops on me, I stopped for a second and asked her how she was. Pretty good, she said, bending her head down and taking a sip of her coke. It made me sort of ill, just how good-looking she was. She asked me how it was going and I started to tell her, I mean I started to say that everything was okay, but it didn't sound very interesting, I was afraid she was going to bugger off, so I said I had a little problem, my parents had gone away for the weekend and I'd thrown a great big party and now the house was a mess, there were stains on the carpet and I was sort of in trouble.

"What sort of stains?" she asked.

"Oh, you know," I said, all mysterious, implying, I guess, that there'd been some great big fucking orgy and there were like shot spots all over the house. I couldn't shut up. And the funny thing is, she sort of listened and made suggestions, you know how to get the carpet clean, add some, I forget what, something and cold water and a sponge, but really, while I was talking, I had this sensation, it was just hanging over me like a cloud of dread, that maybe I was coming across like a big fat creep, or just the biggest fucking liar in the history of mankind.

"I think one of them might have had her period as well," I said, going completely into orbit.

"You mean there was more than one?"

"Just the first night," I said.

Even after that she didn't leave. The band came back on, and we kept talking, you know, how to get my house clean, and it was getting bigger and more complicated. Finally a slow song came on. I looked over the railing and I said, get this, "Nice song."

Great eh?

And she said, "Yeah."

And I said, "It's nice to dance to this stuff."

"Yeah," she said.

"But I don't like asking people to dance."

I mean obvious or what.

She gave her drink a final little slurp and put it on the floor against the railing.

"I'll dance with you," she said. So we went down the stairs and out onto the floor, everybody sees me with this great-looking chick, and she put her hand up on my shoulder and I put my hand on her back, I could feel the sweat coming through her shirt, and I could smell her perfume, it didn't smell like great perfume, sort of like the cheap stuff, as my mother would say, but I liked it just fine.

And at the end of the dance she kind of stepped back, like she was going to tell me she should go find her sister, you know the number, but I didn't want it to end like that, me leaving the dance figuring she'd got to know me a bit and then split. So real quick, before she could say anything, I said, "Thanks for the dance," and then I spun around and walked off. I mean maybe I looked like a madman but I didn't want to end up feeling like a loser. Not when everything was going so well. Let her wonder a bit, I thought. It's always the guys who do the wondering. Besides, that way when she saw me next Saturday, she'd know I was all right, it was cool to say hi to me, I wasn't going to latch onto her like a fucking lamprey for the rest of the night.

I beetled on out of there. Harper was hanging around outside on the patio.

"Let's split," I said.

And he said, "Well, not yet."

We stayed out there for awhile, bitching about stuff. I made sure not to go back inside. It'd been a pretty good goodbye, I didn't want to water it down with another one.

After awhile, Harper looked around and sort of sucked his lips and said, "Well, maybe we should like *oubliez-la*," which was his way of saying, let's go.

It was around eleven-thirty when we got back to our dock and tied up the boat, Harper sort of laughing about what a shitty night it had turned out to be and me saying, well, what the hell, and then the two of us heading up from the boathouse. We walked up through the swamp, the moon yellow and round, and came out under the stars in the open field and started towards the house. The lights were on in the living room, we could see them from the bottom field, and it made the place look all cosy. Just to freak myself out, I imagined I was a stranger, that I didn't know the people in the house, I'd just been sort of *clonked* there, in the middle of nowhere. You know, what would I do? Would I knock on somebody's door, would I make my way into town? I got so absorbed in thinking about how lonely it'd be out there that I just about jumped out of my pants when Harper spoke to me.

"Did you notice the old lady hid all the guns?" he said, sticking a blade of grass in his mouth.

I caught up to him.

"What?"

"She hid all the guns in the basement."

"What for?"

"The doctor told her to."

"Whose doctor?"

"The old man's doctor."

"Jesus."

"Great eh?"

"Where'd she hide them?"

"Under the stairs, the little place at the back with all the mouse droppings in it. You're not supposed to know, by the way. It's a secret."

"What'd he say?"

"Said he was going to shoot himself."

"Really?"

"He was pissed, I think."

"The doctor was pissed?"

"No, *he* was pissed when he told Mother and *she* told the doctor. Christ, Simon, can't you follow anything?"

"Do you think he'd really do it?"

"No way. You got to have a real pair to stick a gun in your mouth."

"I suppose you're right."

"Well like don't sound so disappointed, Simon. He's your father you know."

"So you don't figure we should leave the basement door open? Leave a round in the chamber just so he doesn't have to make another trip downstairs."

Harper laughed in amazement.

"Nice talk, Simon. Like real psycho stuff. This family, I mean it. Sometimes I feel like they brought the wrong baby home from the hospital. Everybody here seems so *warlike*. I don't think I'm going to be happy until I'm fifty. I've always thought that. Even when I was a kid."

He went quiet for a moment. "I wonder why Annie Kincaid wasn't there tonight?"

We went into the house. He went up to his bedroom and lay on the bed and turned on the radio and listened to a baseball game.

I went downstairs, made myself a ham sandwich. Then went out the back door and swatted deer flies in the garage. They were big as bolts. You had to hit them really hard to bring them down off the window. Sometimes I had to finish them off with my shoe, all buzzing around on the floor and pissed off. It made a sound like stepping on a small light bulb.

Then I went out into the driveway and threw stones into the ravine; across the valley a dog barked from the Barrigers' farm. A car drove along the small road on the horizon. It was very lonely out there, and I came back inside and went upstairs. I looked into Harper's room, but he wasn't very talkative. He was lying there on his bed with his hands behind his head, staring up at the ceiling. From a small maroon radio on his left, the ball game jerked along and halted.

"What do you suppose happens to all those golf balls down in the ravine? I mean do you think they just *disintegrate*?" I said.

"I've got to listen to this," he said. "I'll talk to you later."

I went on down the hall to my room, got onto my bed and opened my book. I was reading a James Bond novel, I can't remember which one, but I flipped ahead to make sure there were enough pages left for the racy stuff.

It must have been after one in the morning when the phone rang. I raced along the hallway in my socks, down the wooden stairs. I took it in the kitchen.

"Hello," I said.

"I hope I didn't wake you up."

"Scarlet?"

"Jesus, you do have a good memory. What are you doing?"

"I was just at a dance."

"Oh yeah?" she said.

"Yeah."

"Meet anybody interesting?"

"Yeah. Well, not really. You know, the usual stuff. What are you doing?"

"My parents are away."

"Oh yeah? They on holiday?"

"No, they're in Los Angeles. My dad's got a couple of movies opening."

"Really?"

"Yeah. He's got to look after the movie stars. Make sure they don't get too drunk. That kind of stuff."

"Oh yeah? Who's he have to look after?"

"Well, I think he's going to have dinner with Steve McQueen. Do you know him?"

"*Have Gun, Will Travel*?"

"No, that's what's-his-name."

"Right."

"Anyway, they're going to have dinner."

"Just the two of them?"

"No, there'll be other people there. I met Alfred Hitchcock once. When I was a kid."

"Really?"

"Yeah."

"What's he like?"

"Not very interested in kids."

She yawned. Then after a pause, "You're not one of those guys, are you? Keeps a lay book?"

"What's a lay book?"

"It's where you write down all the girls you've laid. You know, two stars for a feel, four stars for a home run."

"Hardly."

"I go to a French school," she said. "In Quebec. I almost got kicked out last year. But they let me back in on account of my father."

"What for?"

"This stuff got wrecked and I got blamed for it." You could hear she wasn't interested in going on about that.

"So you're not mad at me for calling?" she asked.

"No, not at all. How'd you know my parents weren't here?"

"I didn't."

"Well, what if they'd've answered the phone?"

"I would've hung up."

"Oh."

"I'm not *stupid* you know."

Silence. "So your parents are away?"

"Yep. I'm just here with my brother."

"Just the two of you?"

"Yeah."

"You should come down here."

"I should. That'd be fun."

"No, I mean it."

"Like when?"

"Like now. Right now."

"What do you mean?"

"Come down here right now. We could stay up all night."

"I don't mean to sound like a bonehead here, but how exactly would I get down there? Just for technical information."

"I don't know. Hitchhike."

"At this time of night?"

"Sure, there's bound to be people up. Truck drivers and stuff."

"Are you putting me on?"

"No."

"Jesus, I don't know, Scarlet. What if I get kidnapped?"

"You're so conservative. It'd be fun."

"I don't think that's my style."

"No, maybe not."

"Well give me the address. Just in case. But I'm not promising. I've got a lot of stuff to sort out up here first."

"Like what?"

"Just stuff. Personal obligations and things. But it's not very likely."

"If you were really daring, you would."

"What if I don't get a ride?"

"I'd pick you up. Anybody in their right mind would pick you up." Another pause. "You could sleep in my father's bed. It's as big as a tennis court. With satin sheets."

"It'll take hours."

"I'll be up."

"Yeah?"

"Just ring the buzzer. You'll see."

"So?" she said after a moment.

"I'll try."

"Don't say you'll try. People always say they'll try and nothing ever happens."

"All right. I'll really try."

"You better."

"I will."

"Aren't you forgetting something?"

"What?"

"The address."

So she gave it to me.

After I put down the phone I just sat there for a minute, moving my jaw from side to side. It made a funny sound in the middle of my head. I always did that when I was thinking about something, but Harper said it made me look like a fish with a hook in his mouth so I only did it in private. I went upstairs to his bedroom. The wallpaper was light blue in there. He had a football balanced on his chest.

"Was that that broad again?"

"Yeah."

"What'd she want?"

"She wants me to come down and see her. Tonight."

"Right," he said.

I went down the hall and sat on my bed. Then I got up and looked at myself in the mirror. I hauled out my wallet and looked inside. I had a whole lot of cash the old lady had left, just in case of an emergency. *I could do it*, I thought, *I really could*. I could feel it going from a wild idea to something I might actually do, I could actually feel it happening inside me, like a lab experiment, fizz, fizz, all the chemical stuff mixing together.

Finally I got up off my bed and I went back into Harper's room. I stood in the doorway.

"I think I'm going to," I said.

"What?"

"I think I'm going to go."

"You can't. I'll get in shit. The old lady will blame me."

"I'll be back in time."

"Forget it."

I started down the hall. I heard him get off his bed. I ran down the stairs, taking them two at a time, giggling like a maniac, and burst out the side door and started up the driveway. Just when I got about halfway up, I heard the screen door come flying open.

"Asshole!" he shouted. But I kept going.

I hurried up the dark driveway toward the main highway. I could hear the stream gurgling behind the trees. Stones scattering under my feet. Man, was I wide awake.

I got to the top of the road and started to walk toward town. In the moonlight I could see all the way across the fields. There were no cars. I must have walked for about fifteen minutes, everything still as a graveyard when I heard this funny humming sound. I stopped and listened. Way at the far end of the road, a pair of headlights came swinging around the corner and came up toward me like a shotgun. I put out my thumb, shielding my eyes. They got closer and closer, they were really coming down on me, the guy blasted his horn and then roared by, this great big wind flapping my clothes like I was some kind of scarecrow.

Then everything was still again.

I kept on; I walked by a farmhouse. A dog barked. I jumped. I moved into the centre of the road, walking on the single line, one foot after the other, sticking my arms out for balance, talking to myself a mile a minute. They would have stuck me in the booby hatch if they'd heard. It was like there were six people with me. Me talking to Harper and to my mother and then Scarlet, even some of the guys at school, explaining to them what I was doing in the middle of the road in the middle of the night. They were all ears.

Another car came winding around the corner. I stood way back from the highway this time, a friendly little smile on my face so they didn't figure I'd just taken an axe to my whole family. Just seconds before the guy pulled even with me I felt this weird impulse to throw myself in front of the car.

The guy whizzed by, looking sort of startled. But about a half-mile up the road, his back lights went bright red and just hung there for a second, like a space ship.

Holy fuck, I thought, he's stopped, and I started running toward him. A man in a farmer's hat leaned over and pushed open the door.

"I almost didn't see you," he said. "I'm going into town. How far you going?"

"I'm going to the city."

"I can get you started."

It was stuffy in the car, it smelt like old men and oil and rags.

"Smoke?" he said, offering me a cigarette.

"Sure," I said. I put it in my mouth and he lit it with the car lighter.

"So what are you doing out *here*?"

"I'm going to see my girlfriend."

"Same old story, isn't it?" he said. "Never changes."

We started up, the road snaking through the black countryside. A deer ran into the bush. A song came on the radio, real slow, country and western, normally stuff I hate but tonight I was kind of in the mood.

I saw you tonight
In her arms so tight
I watched as she held you tenderly.

The guy turned it up. We drove through town. A police car was sitting in the empty gas station. The farmer took me to the outskirts.

"Good luck," he said and drove off.

I got another ride. Can't remember where he dropped me off. Just a bunch of pictures, a waitress in a pink dress staring from a truck-stop window. That soft light off the radio in the dashboard. It was like I kept hearing the same song all night long.

I don't want to go out
But I can't just stay home
I don't need company
But I sure don't want to be alone.

I got out of one car and into another. At four o'clock in the

morning, I was standing at an amber-lit intersection on the outskirts of another town. A sixteen-wheeler picked me up.

"Hang on kid," the driver said, "we're going all the way to
Toronto."

It was quarter past six when I got to the front door of Scarlet's
place. Into the lobby. Real bright; smelt like perfume and that
potpourri shit. Carpets, chairs, vases, lamps, a wonder somebody
didn't make off with all that stuff in the middle of the night.

I rang Scarlet's number. It took awhile.

"Guess who?" I said.

There was this squawk from her end of the line. The door
buzzed and I pulled it open. When I got out of the elevator,
Scarlet was sort of peeking out the door.

"Jesus Christ," she said. "You actually came."

She was wearing a fluffy white dressing gown.

"Whoa," she said, leaning against the doorframe. "I've got
to lie down. I got up too fast. I'm seeing stars."

I caught a glimpse of the light coming in the windows down
the hall, and for some reason it made me think about studying
for my Physics exam.

I followed her into her bedroom. It was dark in there, the
curtains pulled, and it smelled like a girl's room. I sat on the edge
of the bed.

"So what do you want to do now?" I said.

"You talk and I'll sleep," she said. "I'm not very good in the
morning."

"Really?"

"Don't be disappointed. I'm just going to have a little rest
here. Tell me something. Talk to me."

She put her hands under her head.

"You know that guy at the party," I said, "the one you were kissing on the mouth?"

There was a little bit of silence.

"Are you sure you want to talk about that now?"

"Who *was* that guy?"

"A friend of the family."

"You can say that again."

"I mean I've known him since I was little. It was his birthday, so I gave him a kiss. Big deal."

"But you felt pretty guilty about it. I could tell."

"I was afraid you were going to snitch on me."

"No, I wouldn't do that."

"Were you jealous?"

"Now why would I be jealous? I hardly knew you."

"For some guys, that's all it takes."

"Yeah, well, I'm not some guys."

I looked around the room. "It smells nice in here. What's that smell? It's like vanilla."

"You like that?"

"Yeah."

"I like it too. It's exotic."

She was quiet for a moment.

"God, I wondered when you were going to bring that guy up. You probably thought I was a big whore."

"Actually, it's pronounced the other way. Like the moving company."

"Simon, it's too early for grammar lessons. Really. I feel sort of sick to my stomach. Why aren't you tired? Lie down here for a minute. Just be quiet."

I went over and lay down on the very edge of the bed. She turned over and faced the wall.

"I've always wondered what it would be like to sleep in a pink room," I said after awhile.

"Shhh," she said.

I lay there and tried to sleep.

"I can feel you thinking, Simon. It's making the whole bed shake. What are you thinking about?"

"Snakes."

She didn't answer.

"When I was a little kid," I went on, laughing all of a sudden, nerves probably, "my mother used to come in and tuck me in and sometimes she'd say, 'Well, Simon, what do you want to talk about?' and this one time, I thought for a second and I said, 'Snakes.' I must have been about six, but I remember that very clearly. Not the other times. But that one. Weird eh?"

She rolled over and looked at me. Very pretty. Didn't say anything, just looked at me.

"What?" I said, suddenly very self-conscious.

"In the dark, you're very handsome."

She rolled back over again. I lay there, looking at the back of her neck. You could see where her hair had been chopped; it was thick and then nothing, just her neck. From that angle, I was thinking you couldn't tell if she was a boy or a girl. Except for the smell, of course. No guy ever smells like that. Or should anyway. So I lay there for awhile longer, thinking about this and that, the way you do, but really thinking about one thing, the other stuff just jumping along the surface like grasshoppers. I put my hand on her shoulder, really softly, so it was hardly there. But she didn't move or twist around, didn't do anything that told me to move it. So I let it rest there, the full weight of my hand, this ache in my arm, I realized, from the tension of holding it there, a very unnatural position. But she didn't move away. And then I moved my face right close to the back of her neck and I kissed her hair. But I could tell by her breathing that she wasn't quite asleep yet. There's a way people breathe when they sleep and a way they breathe when they're waiting for something. I didn't really know her well enough to be sticking my tongue in her mouth and besides I wasn't sure I tasted too good, so I sort of hugged her. But really gently. I had the feeling, you know, that I was a safe-cracker, I was opening a very, very expensive safe, one false move would set off the alarms and release the dogs. So I proceeded very carefully. Very carefully, I pulled her shoulder toward me. It gave a little. I tugged a little harder and she just rolled over, her eyes still shut and her face in my armpit now. All warm and sleepy but not quite asleep. I started moving my hips a little bit, they just started moving themselves actually until I felt myself being drawn toward this giant, black planet. I could feel it drawing me toward its surface until gradually it seemed sort of inevitable that I'd go there; suddenly all the nerves in my body switched direction and I could feel myself arrive somewhere that was absolutely *me*.

CHAPTER THREE

SLEEPING in the same bed with somebody ain't all it's cracked up to be though. I mean you want it to be nice for them, you know, not breathing all over them or lying on your back snoring like something that's been washed up on a beach. You can't really relax, just let one go like you might in your own bed; on top of which I'd taken my shirt off, it always makes me sweat wearing clothes when I sleep, but I was having a little breakout on my back, too many chocolates, and so I was self-conscious about turning over. In case she could see. So the ideal position was me lying with my arm over her, her facing the wall, which was fine but I like to flip around a lot, not to mention go to the bathroom a half-dozen times, so all in all I didn't have the world's best sleep. At one point I rolled over and I felt this thing under my hip. I reached down and pulled it out; it was a stuffed animal, a skunk I think, it was in the bed with her like she was a little girl. I looked at it for a second. I almost laughed but then I had second thoughts. So I slipped it back under the covers and the three of us sailed off to sleep again, me, Scarlet and the little skunk.

Sometime around eight, I remember because I looked at the clock in the hall on the way back from the can, I lay down on the floor beside the bed. Scarlet was sound asleep, and I didn't want to wake her. I wasn't quite ready for everything to start up. I closed my eyes and boy, did I go under fast. Wow. Like I'd been crowbarred.

Next thing I knew, something moved in the room. I opened my peepers; there was Scarlet stepping over top of me, a sheet wrapped around her, like an Italian movie star or something.

I woke up God knows how much later. I lay there for awhile on the floor, looking around the room, feeling pretty pleased with myself, I have to tell you. I mean, like, I did it. I actually fucking did it. Just imagine what my little audience on the highway would have made of this, me making it all the way down here and then spending the night with a girl.

I scrambled into my jeans and shirt and came out in the living room, the sun blazing down, me doing up my shirt pretty fast on account of my chicken chest. Sometimes in the shower I imagine people staring at me because I'm so skinny. Sometimes I tell them I've been sick recently. Ill, that's the word I use. Sounds more tragic.

"Jesus H. Christ," I said. "It sure is bright out here. Man, I can hardly see."

Scarlet was sitting in a big chair with her legs draped over the side; wearing a white T-shirt and blue shorts. And glasses with big brown frames.

She whipped them off.

"About time," she said.

I didn't want to get too near her on account of not having brushed my teeth.

"Great view," I said, standing in front of the window. "You must never feel like you're missing anything. Nothing going on out there without your permission."

"God you talk a lot."

"Is it too much?"

"What?"

"The talking."

"No, I like it."

"Can I borrow a toothbrush?"

"Use mine, it's the one with the blue handle."

"I'll wash it off with soap when I'm done."

"That's okay," she said. "I'll survive."

I went into the bathroom. I found the brush in a plastic glass with a few others. I ran my thumb along the bristles. I could feel a small spray of water; I didn't rinse it off; call me a pervert, whatever, I just liked the idea of putting it in my mouth when it was still wet from hers.

I came out of the bathroom, brush in my mouth, lather all over the place, scrubbing away like mad. I started to say something.

"I can't understand a word you're saying," she said.

"What?"

"I can't make out what you're saying."

I pulled the brush out of my mouth. I sounded like those deaf guys you see in the subway, flapping their hands about and making funny noises.

"I was saying that I have a clock in my head. It's the strangest thing. Day or night, I know exactly what time it is. Like not sort of, or approximately. I mean right on the buzzer."

"What time is it now?"

"Well, I can't do it when I'm self-conscious. I've got to sort of sneak up on it. I'll tell you later. When I'm not trying."

She made me a piece of toast and buttered it. I don't generally eat around girls. Too many opportunities to be unattractive. Scarlet, I noticed, ate with her mouth open, just a bit, not gross, but you'd have thought her parents would have jumped on that one. I can't even say "anyways" without my mother making a fuss. It may seem mean but it sort of relaxed me seeing Scarlet do stuff wrong.

"Start," she said, pointing to the toast.

"I can also tell the future," I said.

"Like, for example, what?"

"Well, for example, sometimes I know the phone's going to ring. So I pick it up. I even know who it is. I inherited it from my mother, she's psychic. I called her once from Vancouver. She picked up the phone and said, 'Hello, Simon,' just like that. She hadn't seen me for three weeks."

"So do you know what's going to happen to you and me?"

"No. But I knew you'd call."

"Liar."

"I did."

"*I* didn't even know."

"Well, I did. I wasn't surprised at all. Couldn't you hear that, me not being surprised?"

"You sounded pretty excited."

"Well, I'm always like that. But that's not the same as surprised."

"So when you know what's going to happen to you and me, will you tell me?"

"Sure."

"Even if it's bad?"

"Especially if it's bad."

I figured it was time to quit while I was ahead and stop talking. So I did. And ate my toast.

"I don't usually eat in the morning," I said, which was a king-size whopper, I eat like a wolf all the time. Even more than my brother, which makes my skinniness something of a mystery.

Scarlet lit a cigarette. You could see by the way she held it, hardly noticing, that she'd had a cigarette before in the morning. The smoke floated across the room to me. I liked the way it smelt. This is a different league, I thought. People smoking in their house like it's no big deal.

"Do your parents let you smoke in the house?"

"Depends."

"On what?"

"On what kind of mood they're in."

"My mother gets me to light her cigarettes for her when she's driving."

"Do you want one?"

"Sure."

She watched me light up.

She sort of grinned and looked out the window.

"What?" I said.

"You look like you don't smoke. The way you hold it."

"How does it look?"

"Sort of *feminine*."

"Really?"

A bit later, I called my brother.

"Hey, Harper," I said, "it's me."

"Where are you?"

"I'm at Scarlet's."

"Fuck man, you got to get back here. The old lady called this morning. She wanted to fucking talk to you."

"What'd you say?"

"I said you were down at the dock. But she's coming home tomorrow. So you better get back here."

"I'm coming."

"When?"

"Tonight."

"For sure?"

"For sure."

There was a pause and I heard him take a bite of apple.

"So you guys up all night?"

"I got a bit of sleep."

"Her parents still away?"

"Yep."

"She there?"

"Yep."

"Like right beside you?"

"Yep."

He hung it there for a moment, then he changed gears.

"Cool. But don't fuck me on this one."

"No sweat," I said.

I was feeling a whole lot better, relieved really, when I put down the phone. I don't like people being pissed off with me, even if I'm in the right. It nags at me. Anyway. We set out for downtown. It was pretty lively outside. Warm breeze, people walking around. Saturday is always a great day in the city. A subway train roared by above ground, I looked over, and I had one of those funny feelings that I was going to remember that moment for the rest of my life. Weird, those times, they just stick in your bean like a photograph, not the moment before, just that one, and not always because something's going on. Sometimes it's nothing at all, like a train roaring by, and Scarlet just standing there, her hair not quite touching her shirt collar.

We walked along Eglinton Avenue, past the bike shop where the old man bought me my first gear bike. Me talking away, I mean just incapable of shutting the fuck up. On the other side of the street, just down a bit, was the Apple Paradise. I used to go there with my neighbour Kenny Withers on a Saturday night and get a great big gooey dessert, one of those apple monsters with maple syrup and whipped cream, the kind of shit kids like. Funny to think we were happy doing nothing more than going out and getting a fancy apple and then going home and watching the hockey game. Hard to imagine something like that could make anybody happy. No girls, nothing. Just an apple.

I pointed out a couple of these historical landmarks to Scarlet, like they were famous battlefields or something. Even the giant rock in the little parkette where Daphne Gunn dumped me. I told her about how she took me out there one night right after dinner—instead of inviting me into her house, always a bad sign—sat me down on this big rock, and gave me the old axeroo. I walked home like a zombie, it was like I was marching to my death, up the street, in the door, up the stairs, into my bedroom, flopped onto my bed, eyes staring at the ceiling, waiting for something to happen. For it all to end I suppose. Like one of those deer shot in the heart that keeps running, doesn't know it's dead yet. Yikes. Not a place I'm keen on returning to. But the funny thing was that if I'd only known that down the road things'd turn out all right, you know, me here with a beautiful girl, all that back there, so far back it was fun to think about, even the grisliest part, well if I'd only known all that, I wouldn't have been so upset. Man, that sure would have blown Daphne's mind, her giving me the axe and me popping up like a piece of fresh toast, saying sure, I understand, you're right, and wandering off home, hands in my pockets, even whistling a tune. Boy, that would have surprised her. But I didn't know enough. I just walked on home with my head in my hands like a basketball and cringed for the next three months every time somebody brought up her name. Yeah, I sure handled that one. Next time, I thought to myself, I'll know better, I'll just remember today, how everything worked out in the end and I won't have to go through that bullshit again.

"Do you think I'm beautiful?" Scarlet said all of a sudden.

"What? Are you kidding?"

"No, I'm not."

"Yeah, you sure are. You make guys nervous. I mean I didn't even want to *think* about talking to you at my party."

"What'd you think I'd do?"

"Tell me to buzz off or something. Wouldn't have surprised me a bit. Some girls, when they're really pretty, it's the weirdest thing. They make me feel like I'm *shorter* than they are. You were scary, man."

"Yeah?"

"And I'm not just saying that."

"Am I less scary now?"

I could see we were headed for possible trouble here.

"Well it's not like I got you or anything. If that's what you mean."

"No, I knew I liked you right away. The second I saw you. You sort of reminded me of myself."

"I remind you of yourself? Jesus, this I got to hear."

"I'd probably be like you if I was a boy."

"Gee, I don't think so, Scarlet. I think you'd be like one of those guys in the hallways, you know, in the coolest clothes, button-down shirts and continental pants. There's a whole cluster of them hang out in front of prayers every morning."

"No, I'm not like that at all. You don't know me very well."

She stopped in front of an ice cream store and peeked in the window.

"Do you want an ice cream cone?" I said.

"My mother thinks my nose is too blunt."

"Your mother told you that? That's a weird thing for a mother to do. They're only supposed to tell you the good stuff."

"What does your mother tell you?"

"My mother tells me I have a sensuous mouth."

"Oh yeah?"

"That I will be an excellent kisser."

"Really," she said. And then she turned her head to the side and said something that I didn't quite catch.

"What?" I said, but she didn't answer and I knew not to push it. I was just about bursting with pleasure though. Funny thing about that expression, "seeing red": it's supposed to be when you're pissed off. It's just the opposite with me. When I'm happy things go kind of strawberry.

"Do you?"

"Do I what?" I said.

"Think my nose is too blunt?"

"No."

"Look at it."

"I think you look like a movie star. I don't know what I'd do if I was as good-looking as you. I don't think I could stand it. I'd be going over to the mirror every fifteen minutes. I mean I do that anyway, I keep hoping something will change between trips."

"If I saw you on the street, I'd think, that's a nice-looking person."

"Yeah?"

"A friend of mine said you were going to be a real doll when you grew up," she said.

"Who was that?"

"I'm not supposed to say."

"But really, she said that?"

"Yep. But don't let it go to your head."

"I won't."

I waited a moment.

"You're sure she meant me?"

"Sure I'm sure. She named you by name."

It's true what they say; you never notice fuck-all until you're doing it yourself; you get a puppy, suddenly you see all the dogs in the world; it's the same for couples, suddenly, they're every-where. Like all over the place, even the Chinese, everybody just *doing* it. Like it's the only game in town. Which come to think of it, it is. But I'm telling you, it was like waking up in a totally new country.

"Let's steal something," Scarlet said.

"Forget it."

"Why not?" she said, sort of peeved.

"Because I don't want to get caught. Because I don't want to get wheeled down the driveway of my summer cottage in the back of a squad car in handcuffs."

"You remember in that movie, when they go in and steal something?" she said.

"I didn't see that movie."

"Well you should have. It was a really good movie."

"What do they steal?"

"Doesn't matter. It's just something they do together be-cause they're in love."

"Maybe you got more guts than me," I said, sucking up a bit. "I'm scared of getting caught. Aren't you scared of getting caught?"

"I've been caught before," she said. "My father thought it was a big fat joke."

"My father'd slug me."

"If my father ever laid a hand on me, I'd stick a knife through him like a bug."

I sort of looked at her twice when she said that. I wanted to tell her to simmer down, there was nobody in our immediate vicinity who deserved to die for fucking around with her, not so far today anyway, but I figured that'd piss her off even more. Whatever it was, it changed the climate just like that, on a dime, and for some reason my heart started beating fast like I was in trouble or something.

We passed by a pet store. There was a little bowl of goldfish swimming in the window.

"What's your father in the loony bin for?" she asked.

"For being an asshole. They've got a special wing for those people. My family are charter members."

Funny thing is, as I said it, I felt a sort of spear go through me, shame or something, as if, like in those cartoons, right up at the corner, I could see my old man listening to me talking about him like that. It actually made me wince. I mean, sure, he was an asshole (a bully mostly), but he was more than *just* an asshole. But you wouldn't have known that from listening to me. Sometimes I think I'll say anything about anybody just to get a laugh. It's pretty disgusting.

"You should come up to our summer cottage," she said.

"I didn't know you guys had a cottage."

"My father rents it. It's up in Georgian Bay. He goes there with his show-business buddies and they all get pissed for a week."

"So what do you do?"

"Nothing. Wander around the rocks. Look at the water. Go down to the dock. Scratch mosquito bites. We don't even have a TV."

"Maybe you should take up drinking."

"I already do that. Drinking and masturbating."

"Jesus, Scarlet."

"Well really," she said, laughing, "there's nothing else to do up there."

"Don't you know anybody up there?"

"Look who's changing the subject. And look whose face is turning red, *Mr Beetman*. What's the matter? Cat got your tongue? That's got to be a first. How do you spend *your* time up at your cottage? Fishing and water-skiing and all that cottage crap?"

"Well I don't spend it doing *that*."

"Not at all?"

"No."

"Never?"

"Never."

"Liar, liar, pants on fire."

We walked on for a little while.

"Sometimes I do it in front of the mirror," she said.

"Jesus Christ, Scarlet," I said, "will you *cool* it?"

But you could see she was real pleased to have got that in.

Just to get her off the subject, I went into one of those discount clothing stores. It was nice and cool in there, old ladies shopping for lingerie or pants for their retarded sons, I don't know, but we just drifted along from aisle to aisle, picking stuff up and putting it back until we got a house detective standing so close to us that we scooted out the other side and back into the sunshine. By now I was pretty hungry so we went into Fran's on St Clair. I must have been getting pretty easy with Scarlet because this time I didn't mind eating in front of her. Even a big messy cheeseburger with the cheese dripping down the side, her sitting on the other side of the booth, her feet up, leaning against the wall smoking a cigarette.

"I got to go back to school in five weeks," she said. "Fuck."

The waitress came over and asked her to put her feet down.

"Sorry," she said. When the waitress went away, she put them right back up.

"Do you think I have nice legs?"

"Yeah. Sure."

"I'm not so sure. I think they're too thick at the bottoms."

She took a puff on her cigarette.

"How come you're not with Daphne Gunn any more?"

"We broke up."

"Do you still like her?"

"No."

"It's all right if you do you know. Like I don't own you. Everybody's got something to hide."

"Well it's certainly not Daphne Gunn. She looks like a fucking potato. Like I'm not going to stagger through life all scarred up just because Daphne Gunn dumped me."

"So she dumped you?"

"In a manner of speaking."

"I bet you'd like to get her back."

"I never think about it."

"Yes you do. Too bad we couldn't run into her right now, make her real jealous. That'd be fun wouldn't it?"

I didn't say anything.

"Admit it," she said. "It'd be fun."

"All right, it'd be fun."

"Next time she's at a party, tell me. I'll make a big fuss over you right in front of her."

She took a puff on her cigarette. "I love getting even with

people. That's the thing about me. I'm very patient you know. Like I'll wait years if I have to. But then, just when they think they're safe, I pounce. Like that."

"Sounds a little mental to me."

"I'm just more honest than most people."

She watched the waitress walk by the table.

"I got a bad temper," she said. "You don't want to cross me."

Sometimes there's stuff people like about themselves that's supposed to be bad; but you can tell by the way they talk about it that they think it's neat. I could tell somebody must have told her once she had a bad temper and she liked how it made her sound.

I finished my burger. Suddenly, all the food hitting my stomach made me go kind of glassy-eyed.

"Boy, I'm bushed," I said.

"Did I just bore the shit out of you?"

"No."

"You look bored."

"How do I look bored?"

"You're staring at things. That's what I do when I'm bored. Sometimes it's a person on the subway. Like a man or something and he thinks I'm giving him the eye. That's how dumb some guys are."

"I got to get out of here," I said. "Otherwise I'm going to land in my ketchup."

But just then a couple of guys from school walked by, outside the window. Normally I wouldn't say fuck-all to them, they belonged to a totally different group, guys who took the bus, they lived in parts of Toronto that sounded like different cities, and I always felt a bit sorry for them, being so far from the action and all. But today I waved. One of them, a nice guy with curly hair,

Chummer Farina (now where'd he get a name like that, no wonder he lived on Mars), turned around and saw Scarlet. He said
something to his pal, who had an equally weird name, and then
they both turned around and looked at her, which pleased me a
great deal. I imagined they were talking about it as they went away.
But you know, that's the thing with me. I figure people are walking around all day thinking about me. I mean the fact that I hardly
ever think about them or when I do it's for like a split second,
well, you'd think that might discourage me. But no, it doesn't.

We got back to her place near six. I was pooped. I hadn't got
a lot of sleep and after I ate a sandwich (I couldn't stop eating
now), I fell asleep on the couch. I woke up feeling like you do
when you go to sleep in daylight and wake up in the dark, sort
of bonkers. I had a terrible taste in my mouth, too. So I went
into the bathroom and used her toothbrush again and threw
some cold water on my face. When I came out she was sitting
by the window, looking out over the city. It was a mighty pretty
night, everything just twinkling and you couldn't hear anything, it was like being in a huge aquarium. We just sat there for
awhile, staring out.

"Do you think you're going to be famous?" I asked.

"I don't know. Maybe," she said.

"A famous model?"

"No, my legs are too short."

"I think I'm going to be famous," I said.

"How do you know?"

"I think I look at things like a famous person would look at
them."

"That's a bit conceited."

"I don't go around telling people. That would be conceited."

"You just go around *thinking* it. That's worse," she said.

"But I think feeling famous is part of what makes you famous."

We stared out for awhile longer, not looking at each other, the room getting darker and darker.

"But you got to be able to do something special," she said after awhile. "Like be able to sing or something."

"I know."

"So what can you do?"

"I don't know yet. But there must be something. Otherwise it'd be a super cruel joke to feel like this."

"My father likes famous people," she said. "I think he wishes he was famous himself."

"Everybody wants to be famous."

"No. Not everybody thinks it's a big deal."

"I think you got to be famous to know it's no big deal. Otherwise you're cheating. It's like you're giving yourself an excuse not to try."

"Maybe."

I looked over at her. She was very pretty in that dark room, her head resting on her hand.

"I'm not going to be famous," she said.

"You don't know that."

"No, I do. I'm not good at anything. I'm probably going to end up with somebody famous. That must be why I met you."

It was some kind of day, I'll tell you.

CHAPTER FOUR

I GOT TO THE STATION around nine-thirty that night and sat around down there, waiting for my train. I had plenty of things to think about, but I don't have a lot of patience so I kept getting up and wandering around, looking at the newspapers and the magazines and then going into the coffee shop and then going to have a look at myself in the bathroom mirror and take another pee.

I saw this pretty girl sitting on a bench near me. She looked like a little deer, her hair all short and soft and blond and when her mother went to get something I found myself sort of hoping she'd talk to me. And then I thought, man, I really am a greedy little asshole. Like I just left my girlfriend and here I am, already on the prowl. Anyway she didn't look twice at me (girls don't usually, I've got to talk to them a bit first, otherwise I'm the Invisible Man), and after awhile she went away and I was left alone there, staring up at that high, high ceiling, listening to the names of tiny little towns come floating over the speaker system. Grimsby . . . Fergus . . . Port Dalhousie . . .

I went over and asked the guy for about the ninth time when the train was coming and he finally sent me down to Track Number Two and I climbed aboard. I wanted to be there first, get a good seat. I'm very fussy about where I sit; doesn't matter if it's a movie or a plane ride, I've got to be in just the right place. So I got a seat right next to the aisle so I could get up and take a pee without pissing everybody off. You know, like whenever I wanted to. Of course, once you can, you never have to.

But there was hardly anybody on board, except for an old woman down the aisle eating a sandwich very carefully, eating with these little careful bites like she thought her teeth might break if she chomped down too hard.

A minute later a drunk came wandering through. He had red eyes and a fur hat on and he caught my eye coming into the compartment. I don't know why but I'm an awful magnet for crazy people, they just seem drawn to me. So I've formed a scientific theory to instantly weed them out. I look at their shoes. Crazy people have always got fucked-up shoes. The tongues are hanging out or they're way too big or they're absolutely the wrong colour for the guy who's wearing them, like bright yellow on a bum in a long coat; or they've got elevated heels on them, there's a ton of things to look for. So when I walk down the street, for example, and I see some guy looking through the crowd at me, when I see him make that decision that I'm the guy and start to make a beeline for me, first thing I do is look down and check his shoes.

Which is what I did with the guy on the train. Sure enough, they were fucked-up. No laces.

I could smell him too.

"Hello there, young fellow."

I looked over.

"Oh hello," I said in this real shitty formal voice.

"Can I join you?"

"I'm sorry, you can't. I'm waiting for my mother. She's with the police force."

Well, that last part may have been a bit unnecessary but I threw it in anyway. I knew if I let the guy sit down, he'd be yapping all the way to kingdom come and while normally I don't care who I talk to, tonight was sort of special. Tonight I just wanted to sit in the train and think about all the stuff that happened with Scarlet.

Anyway he split. He was very nice though, which made me feel a bit shitty. He wandered off down the train where no doubt somebody else was going to tell him to fuck off. I wondered if he had any kids. Like could he phone them up and say, "I'm tired of being a drunk. Can I come over?" I sat there daydreaming about this guy going home to his kids, everybody being nice to him, giving him a bath and fluffy towels, the mirror all steamed up; and then him sitting in the living room in a brown dressing gown, having a cup of tea. Little old grizzled face all happy.

Finally we started up, the train lurching out of the station, ugly stuff on both sides, brick and barbed wire. But after awhile we cleared the city limits and picked up speed. It was sort of cool rattling through the countryside, everything all black outside, those little towns going by, thinking about Scarlet, about how yummy her face smelt when it was all wet. Or how she smelt when she was a little bit sweaty and leaned over to grab something. Wow. There was one time when she reached up to bat a spider web off the chandelier and her shirt came out of her jeans and I could see her tummy. I had this overwhelming desire to lean over and lick it like an ice cream cone. She probably would have called the cops on me, thought I was a big pervert, but that's what I wanted to do. It's an amazing thing, when you come right down to it, that girls aren't grossed out by guys, all the disgusting things we want to do to them.

I got into the Hunstville train station near midnight; not much there, just a little shack on the edge of town, down by the planing mill, and a guy in a taxi with the lights off. I went over and he wound down the window.

"You going out to Grassmere?" the guy said.

"Yeah."

"Charge it to your father?"

"Yeah," I said sort of amazed. "How'd you know?"

"Taken you boys out there a hundred times before. Don't you recognize me?"

"Oh yeah. Now I do."

I'm very superstitious and this seemed like a good omen. I hopped in the car. It was like being a foreign prince returning home. Everybody knew me.

Everything was shut up in town, the lights in the movie theatre marquee off. We crossed over the bridge, the wheels making that funny sound on the grid underneath and headed out into the countryside.

"Do you think I could have a cigarette?" I said to the guy. It looked so good him smoking one, it smelt so warm and cosy in the car.

"You don't smoke, do you?"

"Not usually," I said. "But I'm sort of celebrating. I've been away for awhile."

"Oh yeah? Long time?"

"Well, not really. But it seems like a long time. I was in Toronto. Seeing my girlfriend."

"Really?"

"She's a model."

"No kidding. She must be good-looking."

"She is," I said. And then, so it didn't look like I was trying to hog all the glory, I said, "Do you know Toronto?"

"I took my aunt down to the hospital a few years ago. Couldn't get out of there fast enough. If you don't mind me saying."

"I love it." I said. "I'm just made for the place. Like I can't imagine how anybody lives up here."

Once I get talking, Christ only knows what's going to come out of my mouth. "I mean maybe it's an acquired taste," I added. "Maybe I haven't lived up here long enough."

"Well the winters sure are long. That's for sure. Ran Whipper Billy Watson out to his place the other day."

"The wrestler? What's he doing up here?"

"Lives here. Ever since he retired. He grew up around here."

"And he came back?"

"Where would you want him to go?"

"I don't know. I just would have thought being famous and all, he could live anywhere. New York. France, something like that."

"Nope. Told me all he wanted was to get back home."

"Son of a gun," I said. "Whipper Billy Watson. Up here. What's he like?"

"You couldn't ask for a nicer guy. Down to earth. Just like you and me."

"No kidding."

"Like I'm talking to you now."

"Well, I'll be. Whipper Billy Watson."

The lighter popped on the dashboard. I love the smell of a cigarette right after you light it from one of those things. The smoke all blue and moody. You can feel it go right to your head, like a balloon sailing up and bouncing gently off the ceiling, the guy pointing stuff out as we drive, who owns this, who used to own that, who went broke over the winter on account of his drinking, the two of us just shooting the breeze all the way out to the house. It was cool. The whole thing.

You don't want to start behaving like a goof the minute you get a new girlfriend. Nothing drives them away faster than calling them up all the time, putting your mitts all over them, carrying on like a leech. It's like that Sandy Hunter thing. Everything was cool till she turned those lovey-dovey eyes on me, and then I just wanted to jump out the window.

Which is a long way of saying I didn't call Scarlet when I got back to the cottage. I thought about her a lot though, and sometimes in the next couple of days, I really, really wanted to call her, especially at night when I'd been in bed for twenty minutes and started thinking about her sitting in front of the mirror. That was some picture, I'll tell you. I just couldn't get it out of my mind.

But psychology is everything, that's my theory. So I didn't call.

One night, when I was gabbing with my mother in the kitchen, the phone rang.

"So how come you didn't call me?" she asked.

"I didn't want to bug you," I said.

"How would that bug me?"

"You know. Being too available."

"What are you saying? You're not available?"

"Sure I'm available. I just don't want to be a bore about it."

"There's nothing boring about somebody liking you."

"Yes there is," I said.

"You sound like you're speaking from experience."

"I am, sort of."

"Yeah, well there's a difference between being hard to get and being a prick," she said.

"Mostly a question of degree," I said and then laughed, this being an excellent joke.

"You think you're so funny. You're never serious about anything. You should be an actor."

"I don't have the looks for it."

"You don't have to be good-looking to be an actor."

"That's pretty nice, Scarlet."

"That's not what I meant."

"Yes it is."

"It is not. I mean you got to be good-looking to be a movie star. That's not the same thing as being an actor."

"Whatever."

"Let's not get mad at each other, all right? It's just a big waste of time. We'll just end up making up anyway. So let's not do it."

I sat there sort of stunned. She was smarter than I thought.

"So you call *me* next time, all right? I don't want to look like a loser either," she said.

Man, that was a great summer. Harper and me just pissing around, lying on the dock all day getting a tan and then staggering back up to the house, all whacked out from the sun, seeing moons.

On really hot days, when you could hear the leaves rubbing their hands together over your head, we'd take the boat into town, bouncing like crazy over the whitecaps. When you took the engine cover off it sounded like a speedboat.

I always loved that part just before town when you're coming in off the lake, the water's getting shallow, you can see the weeds whizzing by underneath; you go into that channel with the dark, dead logs on the side and the snapping turtles and the wake washing against the river wall and some guy's fishing down there and he pulls his feet up to get away from the rising water.

We'd park the boat at the marina and get her gassed up.

"Charge that to Mr J. P. Albright," we'd say.

Charlie Blackburn, who owned the joint, was a beer-bellied, hard-working guy, and he figured us for spoilt little twerps, driving around in our daddy's boat, not having a job. In fact sometimes I sort of expected him to say no, fuck you. Pay for it yourself, you little prick. But he didn't. Besides, we gave him a lot of business: he fixed up the engine every time we fucked it up. Come to think of it, Charlie was a pretty decent guy. One time, a couple of summers ago, we roared out of the dock with one of the back ropes still tied on, we got about ten yards and boom, everything came to a big stop, we just about went over the bow, miracle the dock didn't come apart. But when things cooled down, the engine sounded sick as a dog, and we took it in to Charlie Blackburn. He took one look at it and said, "What in *hell* did you guys do this time?"

The old man was super steamed when he got wind of it and a week later, when we picked up the boat, he asked Charlie, right in front of us, whose fault it was. Charlie waited a second, he didn't look at us but you could definitely smell the wood burning, and he said, "Just natural wear." I could have kissed the son of a bitch right on the spot. I mean you just never know in this life who's going to surprise you and who's going to fuck you. I mean like never.

We never did much in town, just go up and down the main street about a dozen times; sit on the Town Hall stairs and watch all the people go sweating by; all those girls from summer camp coming through town. Sometimes they'd carry their paddles down the street, just to let you know they were campers out on a long trip. Their bodies all long and brown and their hair a mess. And the local girls, hanging out over by the main dock, smoking cigarettes and wearing make-up in the middle of the day.

Then we'd head back to the marina and hightail it home. Sometimes when I was in that boat, racing over the water, I'd think about Scarlet or a dance that night, and it'd be such a gas, just looking forward to it, knowing it was there, that I'd want to stand up in the boat and shake the steering wheel I was so happy.

But sometimes when I actually *went* to the dance, I'd notice after awhile that nobody was paying any attention to me, the girls looking through me like I was Casper the ghost. It's strange but, even though I had a girlfriend, I found myself wandering around those dances like some kind of orphan, feeling sorry for myself.

Remember the French Canadian girl I told all those whoppers to? The dark-haired one? I ran into her again at Hidden Valley and she asked me to come swimming at her place. She lived in town all year 'round with her sister and her mom. Down by the canal. So I hitchhiked in the next day and when I was going over the bridge, I found myself daydreaming that maybe when I was in the bathroom, changing into my bathing suit, she'd come in the room and start kissing me.

Suddenly I had the unmistakable sensation that I was doing something bad. Exactly like that time in the train station, when I saw the little deer girl. Hoping she'd talk to me. I imagined for a second Scarlet seeing me hurrying over to this other girl's house and really it made me kind of queasy with shame. I sat down on a log. It was still sunny but everything seemed a bit too bright. I looked down beside the log and there was a skinbook there, somebody must have brought it down by the river to jack off. Nice neighbourhood eh? Anyway it was spread open to a picture of this snow-white blond chick with a real rack on her, sort of sitting on a stool in a pair of baby-dolls, but you could see right through them and this rack, just hanging there like something you'd find on a cow. I mean I'd seen girlie pictures before, but this stuff, in view of all the shit I was thinking about, it made the whole world look extremely creepy. Like sex was on everybody's mind and everybody was worth exactly a dollar ninety-eight, including me.

So I started back towards town, like I was a half-decent person, resisting temptation and everything, but then I started thinking about that French Canadian girl coming into the bathroom, me with just a towel around my waist and damn it if I didn't turn around and head back over to her place. God, I was a mess.

Needless to say, it didn't go like my daydream. There were other kids there. And one of them, this local guy, was touching her all the time and not exactly going out of his way to be friendly to me. He was really built, like a weightlifter or something, and he kept jumping off the dock and strutting around with his big muscles and this thing like a fist in his bathing suit. I'm a little self-conscious about my chicken chest and being skinny so I didn't get changed at all. I just sat in the shade with all my clothes on talking to her mother. Hard to believe an old crow like that could have such beautiful daughters, but there you go. Point is, after watching everybody else running around, I found myself feeling sort of shitty, seeing the dark-haired girl and her sister in their bathing suits and thinking I'd never be able to get girls like that. It was like I'd gone in a big circle and ended up back at square one.

So after awhile I got up and left, but as I made my way back along the canal, the depression sort of lifted, it was a nice day again, there were boats puttering along the canal, somebody waved at me from an inboard, I waved back and by the time I got back to the main street I felt fine, thank you very much, just fine.

When I got home I immediately called up Scarlet. She wasn't in so I figured she must be out with some guy. I stewed about it the whole evening, called her like a dozen times until I finally got her old man. He sounded drunk. I figured he wasn't too trustworthy, those boozers can't remember anything, but I left a message anyway for her to call me. It was important. He didn't even know where she was, which pissed me off. Like a great parent or what.

She phoned just before dinner. Soon as I heard her voice I could feel my whole body relax. Still I couldn't help myself.

"So have you seen Mitch?" I said, right out of the blue like a fucking crazy person. I caught a glimpse of myself in the mirror and I looked a little weird.

"No," she said. "Why?"

"I don't know. I just wondered."

"Have you?" she said.

"No, no, like I just wondered, that's all. You know, run into him or something?"

"No," she said, sort of like the queen, "Mitch and I don't travel in the same circles."

But you know, fucked-up as it was, I still felt better, there was something that let go of my chest.

"So is everything okay down there?" I said. "You haven't met anybody or anything?"

"Who would I meet?"

"No one. I was just curious."

"Have you?"

"Hardly," I snorted.

We chatted a bit more and then, feeling a whole lot better, like I'd just finished some huge school project, I put down the phone. Sometimes I think if people could see into my heart, nobody would love me. Sometimes you just can't believe how awful you are. It makes you shake your head.

In the meantime, this great summer just kept on happening. Sometimes we'd go water-skiing with some kids across the lake. Or I'd go snorkelling in the weed beds, the sunlight all golden and religious under water. But it was jumpy down there, you kept expecting something to get you, kept snapping your head around to see if it was there.

Sometimes, Harper and I even played golf. There was this little rinky-dink golf course on the other side of the lake, a nine-holer, and every year the old man took out a membership for us—he wanted us to be golfers just like him. On the way over I saw Donald Glendinning down on his dock. He was varnishing a canoe for his old man, paint brush in his hand, work clothes on, right in the middle of this scorcher. He was always doing stuff like that, Donald, sanding a porpoise board, scrubbing down the boathouse. I always felt kind of shallow when I was with him. Sort of expected that one day down the road I'd open the newspaper and read about him being the prime minister or something. He was just that kind of guy, a winner without being an asshole.

I gave him a big wave.

Anyway, I just don't have the disposition for golf. In spite of my easygoing style, I'm quite a poor loser, and sometimes I'd get so steamed at topping a drive or missing a putt that I'd try to drown my clubs. I mean I'd been right down there by the pond, red-faced, holding a three iron under the water until it saw the error of its ways.

Christ, it was hot there out on the links, the sun beating down. After I was done hacking and slashing I'd make a beeline for the club house, I mean like practically push people out of my way, and buy a cold orange crush. I'd take a few step backwards and throw back my head and just pour this stuff down my throat and I swear to God nothing ever tasted so good. Like I couldn't get my breath, just panting and pouring this shit down my throat.

One morning Harper and I were up at the top of the driveway, shooting the shit and throwing stones into the little stream that ran through our property. We were killing time.

"Hey Harper," I said, "How come there aren't any fish in our stream?"

"It's too little."

"But there aren't even any small fish."

"How do you know?"

"I looked. I used to explore down there."

"Used to pretend you were Davy Crockett?"

For awhile we didn't say anything. The daisies waved in the field and way across the valley, you could see a man walking along the road. Suddenly a cloud passed over the sun and a shadow went racing across the fields.

"It's funny how a cloud changes everything, isn't it?" Harper said. "It's like suddenly there's nothing to look forward to. Like nothing *good* could ever happen under a sky like that."

He looked up the road.

"There he is."

It was the mailman. A white car came around the corner from the junction road and slowed down. The guy stuck his arm out the window with a bunch of letters and a newspaper. I took the hand-off. It was right there on top, a rich looking envelope with the school crest on it. I tore it open on the spot, bits of paper flying in the wind. My eyes shot to the stamp at the bottom of the page, "Promoted to Grade Twelve," and I let out a great big yelp.

English 75, Math 62, History 66, Science 62, Latin 80. Physics 51 (I must have aced the exam!).

Harper shook my hand and gave me a little pat on the back, which was quite demonstrative for him, especially since his report card hadn't come. And then we beat it on back to the house.

I've got one special memory of that summer at the cottage. I was sitting on the porch. It was still morning, you could see the dew on the grass and beyond it the lake all blue and sparkly, it was just another of those weird snapshots burnt into my brain and I knew, I just knew I was happy. Like I caught myself *being* it.

A few minutes later, Harper came downstairs and out on to the patio. He was telling me what he did the night before, met some guys in town and went to the Tastee Freeze where he ran into Annie Kincaid.

"She told me she met a guy she was really nuts about," he said. He gave a sort of unhappy laugh. "So guess I should *oubliez-la.*"

One night I was in the kitchen gabbing away to my mother. I was telling her about that time I pretended I was a pearl diver. I must have been about eleven or twelve and I drove the boat into the middle of the fucking bay and tied an anchor around my waist and jumped over the side. I went down all right, pronto, right to the bottom but when I swam back up there wasn't enough rope, I was three feet short of the surface. I kicked like a son of a bitch, the anchor lifted off the bottom, just enough for me to get a breath and then it pulled me down again.

So there I was, acting out the story in the kitchen when I noticed she'd gone sort of pale; in fact she was starting to look distinctly pissed off and I was getting sorry I'd even brought it up when the phone rang. It was Scarlet.

"I got a job," she said. "At the Exhibition. I'm going to be a still-life model. You pretend you're a statue. People try to make you laugh. I've done it before. It's extremely glamorous."

I didn't say anything about it but that word *glamorous* set me off. Sometimes I had these twisto fantasies about Scarlet, about her cheating on me. They came to me in the stupidest places, at the top of the stairs or looking under the sink, or cutting an orange in half. Like imagining that I turned up unexpectedly at her apartment, real late, and caught her necking with some guy in a car, right out front. It was a green car and they were really going at it. I couldn't see who it was though. His face was in shadow. But it was enough to make me grind my teeth and start talking to myself, just like a mental patient, practising the speech I was going to give her when I caught her. Sometimes I think God's talking to me, you know, like warning me, showing me glimpses of the future. Or maybe the future's already happened and we're all just catching up to it and for some reason I get these special peeks. Other times I think I'm just plain jackrabbit crazy, only a few screw-turns away from being one of those guys shouting at traffic in the morning.

"You don't sound very excited about my new job," she said.

"I am. I'm just tired of being stuck up here."

Which was a funny thing to say since I'd never thought that for a second.

"You should get a job down here. Then we could hang out all the time."

"That'd be great."

"Maybe I could ask my father. He's got connections. He might get you a job in a theatre."

"Like as an actor?"

"No, as an usher."

"I don't know if I'd want to be an usher."

"Why not? You'd get to see all the movies free."

"Yeah. The same one over and over again."

"Well, like no job is perfect. Mine isn't either. It gets pretty boring sometimes."

"That's not how you make it sound."

"Well, I wanted it to sound great, you know. Make all my friends jealous."

"I don't think I'd make anybody real jealous working in a movie theatre. Wearing those stupid little blue jackets. Look like a fucking bellhop."

"It's just an idea."

"I'll think about it."

That night when I went to bed, I thought about Scarlet. I always did, just after I got curled up and closed my eyes. Sometimes she was in her bra and panties, sometimes she was asleep with her hand over her face, other times she'd be sitting on the bed looking at me. Or sometimes she was sitting in front of that mirror, naked.

CHAPTER FIVE

ONE AFTERNOON near the end of July I was out in the garage murdering deer flies when I noticed dust floating over the road, just where it met the main highway. A moment later, a blue Morris came bouncing down the driveway. It came to a stop, a big cloud of gold whirling overtop, the sun shining off the windshield. Still holding the fly swatter I came out of the garage. The door opened. The old man got out. My stomach just sank, like somebody dropped a lead pipe into a river. All things considered, it was just about the worst thing that could have happened, this bomb going off right in the middle of my summer holiday.

But there he was, standing in the driveway, looking pretty good, I have to say, sort of fresh, pants flapping in the wind, hand cocked in a wave. He was happy to be back, you could tell. He must have missed us.

We went inside. The old lady didn't look at all surprised. She must have been expecting him. But it worried me she hadn't said anything. Like maybe it was a surprise. Guess who's back for the *rest of the summer*? I sat around for awhile in the living room, waiting for the verdict. I couldn't very well come out and ask, like, are you here for long? Besides you could see he was making an effort. You know, to be interested, ask questions, even listen all the way through the answers. I made them short, just in case. In spite of myself, I got sort of excited and started offering up a whole lot of stuff, I mean it's more effort to hold yourself in than it is to talk, at least for me it is, so after awhile I was on the edge of the couch, just chatting away a mile a minute. Him nodding like he's giving it real thought. Me rising up for more of it just like a seal after a fish.

"So tell your father about your report card," Mother said, like it was some kind of rare document. But I got to hand it to her. Even when we were little punks she made a fuss over everything we did. Even the littlest, shittiest drawings ended up on the fridge like they were Picassos. After awhile those retardo doodlings started to look interesting even to me. Until I went to the art teacher, a sullen weasel named Vernon Mould, and asked him if I could get in the art programme, and he looked at my little trees going straight into the ground and my psycho school house and said that in his opinion, the art group was pretty much full up.

I went and got the report card off the fridge and showed it to the old man.

"Say, that's pretty good," he said, holding it at arm's length.

Even though I knew it was bullshit, I still couldn't help feeling good. It's your parents, right? They got you by the balls.

"Particularly the physics," Harper came in with. "Talk about clearing the centrefield fence."

"I passed," I said. "That's all that counts."

"A squeaker, if you ask me."

"Well nobody's asking you."

"Harper," Mom said.

"I'm just saying like maybe we shouldn't plan on sending him to MIT."

"We couldn't afford to, anyway," said the old man.

"All right boys," my mother said, "I want to talk to your father for a bit."

I followed Harper onto the driveway.

"What the fuck gives?" he whispered.

"I dunno."

"They didn't let him out, did they?"

"Well he's here."

"Fuck," he said. "Did he bring a whole lot of stuff with him?"

We went over to the Morris, and looked in the back window. There was just a small overnight bag there.

"What do you think?" I looked at Harper.

"Looking pretty good," he said. "If they'd sprung him, he'd have more shit with him."

"Keep your fingers crossed."

So I went back to creaming deer flies, slapping them down off the glass with the fly swatter, giving them the *coup de grâce* with my foot. Crunch. A highly satisfying activity.

After awhile I heard the screen door open behind me. I had a feeling it was the old man but I didn't turn around. I wanted him to watch me for awhile, showing off, I suppose, although come to think of it, it's a pretty weird thing to want to be good at. Killing deer flies. Anyway, finally I turned around.

"Those flies can give you a hell of a bite," he said. "You should put on a shirt. And for God's sake, make sure you don't bust the window."

"I won't," I said. "I'm very careful."

"Does your mother pay you to do that?"

"No. I do it for the sheer pleasure. It's very satisfying."

"Well, as long as you don't break the damn glass."

He looked around the garage, not seeing anything, then put his hands on his hips.

"I think I'm going to go for a bit of a troll."

I sort of sank.

"It's a good day for it," I said.

"Not too windy?"

"Nope." Like I was the expert. Trolling being for me about as excruciating an activity as a human being ever devised. But he was waiting for something, I could tell. "Where you planning on going?"

"Over by the portage, I think."

"That's the deepest part of the lake."

"That a fact?"

"That's what I heard."

"Thought I might gas her up too. Get an ice cream cone."

"I think there's plenty of gas in her right now."

He nodded like that didn't matter. "Listen," he said, "there's something I want to talk to you about. Why don't you come along? Get some fresh air."

Last time he took me somewhere, it was for a little chat about the birds and the bees, this after I'd been dry-docking girls for at least a year. I had to sit there thinking up questions about lesbians so he wouldn't be embarrassed. It just wasn't natural for the old man and me to talk about anything important, my mom did all that stuff, and I didn't like the sound of this. I had a feeling the Clinic shrink had put him up to it. The new improved Dad. It was like a brand new pair of pants he was wearing that didn't go with the rest of him.

The weird thing is that even though he made me nervous (I was scared of him, I admit it), sometimes I also felt protective, like I was the only one in the house who understood him. Knew what he wanted in spite of what he was saying. It was like he was trapped in this old-fashioned sort of British personality—he'd gone to school in England when he was a kid—and sometimes he struck me like an animal stuck in a box, going over and over the same actions to try and get out, even though they didn't work the first time or the hundredth time. So, sometimes, I bent over backwards not to make him feel bad.

Anyway, we set off down through the yellow fields. We found the old road at the bottom and worked our way along it, the old man looking down, thinking of things to say. I think just the effort made it harder, like when you're trying so hard to listen you can't hear a goddamn thing. But he had a nice smile on his face, it was like he was *willing* the whole thing to go well.

We came around the edge of the forest, went up a small hill and turned down through the swamp. The sun disappeared overhead into the tree branches. The air went cool. The mosquitoes came out. We went in single file, him leading, me following. Stepping over tree trunks. It was a spooky place down there; coming home from a dance late at night, it was like something out of a horror movie, the frogs croaking, crickets going creek-creek, creek-creek.

We got to the boathouse, this shitty little red shack on the edge of the lake. Full of mosquitoes and wet bathing suits. Nothing worse than trying to put on a wet bathing suit. Makes your nuts crawl into your stomach. We hauled out the tackle box, a couple of rods, dumped them in the boat and headed out into the middle of the water. It was quite a pretty time of day, late afternoon, the sun setting on the water, everything sort of flickery gold, the old man and me, feeding out our lines, him shading his eyes because it was blinding out there with the sun bouncing off the water. We slowed the engine down to a crawl and then, bringing his rod with him, he came and sat beside me on the front seat.

"I love trolling," he said. "I never catch anything but I love it anyway."

"It's the ritual," I said.

For a moment I thought he hadn't heard me. He was looking way off at the horizon.

"The ritual?" he said with this little frown. A friendly frown though. But like he was puzzled and just a teeny tiny bit irritated to not be sure what I was saying. It made something flutter in me, like *oh-oh, he's getting mad.* I sort of jumped in with my explanation.

"I mean it doesn't matter if you catch anything or not. It's just all the stuff around it. Getting in the boat, being on the water, the company, all that stuff. It doesn't really have anything to do with fish."

"You figure?"

"Yeah," I said. "I used to have that about catching sunfish off the dock. I'd stay down there all day, catching the same fish over and over and over. Eventually I began to recognize his face."

He pulled back on the rod and the line rose from the water, silver drops falling away.

"What do you suppose'd happen if I actually caught something?" he said.

"You'd probably have a heart attack."

I wondered if that was a great thing to say to somebody who'd just been in a clinic for three months.

"I think we're safe," he said.

Things were quiet for a little while. I could feel him working up to something.

"That was a damn fine report card you got, you know."

"Well, I passed. That's a relief."

"You did better than that. Your mother tells me you've turned into a first-rate drummer."

"Did she say that?"

"Verbatim."

"She says I play too loud."

"That's not what she told me. I'd like to come down and hear you sometime."

"I'd be nervous."

"You should get used to an audience."

"It takes me awhile to get warmed up," I said. "You'd have to be patient. And give me lots of warning. And not sneak up on me in case I'm playing a really shitty song."

He frowned.

"I'm sorry, but you know what I mean."

"I'll warn you," he said. "Plenty of warning. You know I used to play the banjo?"

"You did not."

"I did. I had to stop though. Couldn't make the chords any more."

He looked at his left hand. The fingers were bent into a sort of permanent handshake from where a tank hatch fell on them during the war.

"So I hear you have a girlfriend?"

"Yes. A model."

"Never had a model girlfriend. Nice girl?"

"If she likes you."

"Well, does she?"

"Yes."

I waited a moment. "Is that what you meant?" I said.

"Well if I have to ask, the answer is probably no."

It took me awhile to get it.

"Almost," I said.

"Really?" he said. "I had to wait till I got in the army."

"Was that where you met Mother?"

"No, I knew some other gals before your mother."

"Oh."

"It was the war, you know. Kind of a special time."

"It sounds sort of romantic."

"It was, in an odd way."

"I know what you mean," I said.

"Maybe you do."

Way, way off across the lake I could see a tiny tree standing in the middle of a plain. All by itself, miles and miles away. It seemed like another country over there.

We turned the boat into the sun; you could feel the wind shift.

"Are you cold?" he said. "You've got goosebumps."

"No, I'm fine."

"Do you want to go in?"

"No, this is good."

He slowed the boat down even more.

"Listen," he said, "I don't want to embarrass you but there's something I have to say. I'm sorry I've been such a heel. I hope I haven't scared you too much." He gave my arm a little clumsy rub with his hand.

"No," I said.

"Are you sure?"

"Positive."

"Because I haven't been feeling well. Been behaving like a bit of an s.o.b., as we used to say in the army."

"That's O.K."

And suddenly, out of nowhere, I had the strangest desire to burst into tears, right there, like a kid. You could hear it in my voice, it went all wobbly.

"That wasn't very good, putting a fright into a boy like you."

"That's all right, Dad."

"Do you want to go in?"

"I'm fine out here," I said.

And then he turned the boat slowly around into the wind.

We rode on for a little way; then he slowed down the engine almost to an idle.

"We have a bit of a problem on our hands, Simon, and I need you to help me fix it."

"Sure. What?

"Well, it's the house. I don't know if we can keep the whole operation afloat."

"What operation?"

"Well, you two boys in school. And two houses. I think we're going to have to drop something."

"Like what?"

"Well, that's what I wanted to talk to you about. What do you think about selling the house?"

"What house?"

"The city house."

"Gee, that doesn't sound like a very good idea. I like that place."

"You'd stay on at school, of course. Keep your friends, all that. You'd just go as a boarder."

"A boarder?"

"Yes. Nothing wrong with that, is there? I boarded, your Uncle Tom boarded. Not everybody gets to live down the street from their place of education."

Place of education. I didn't like the sound of that. There was a hint of irritation in it, in the tone of voice, and I could feel the old nervousness coming back. I had to be really careful now. Once somebody's scared you when you're little, you stay scared of them, even after you grow up, even after you're bigger than they are. And I could feel that old thing clicking in, like in a second or two he was going to holler at me or give me a cuff across the ear. And even though I could have put up a pretty good scrap now, it didn't matter. I felt like I was still a little kid with this great big black shadow hovering over me.

"I'm a bit old to start into boarding, aren't I? I'm not sure I could get used to it."

"Well you may have to," he said. And something about the way he said it pissed me off, all curt as if I was being a bother, this crap about going into a place that was full of queers, everybody knew it, where they made you go to church every Sunday and they only let you out three Saturday nights a term. I mean it was like a fucking prison compared to being a day boy.

"Is that what you wanted to talk to me about?"

"One of the things."

"I thought we were going to discuss it."

"We are."

"Sounds like you've already made up your mind."

He snorted. "Well, I don't see that we have any choice."

"So we're not really discussing it. I mean it doesn't matter what I say."

"Of course it does."

"But do I have a vote?"

"We don't have enough money for two houses, Simon."

"So I don't have a vote."

I looked away. We putted on in silence.

"Maybe we should go back in," he said. "I didn't realize you were going to be so selfish."

"Selfish?" I said. Whenever you hear that word, *selfish*, you know somebody's just about to stick it to you good. I could feel myself moving someplace I'd never been before, not with him anyway. "You come out here for a talk and when I don't agree to everything you want to go back in."

He looked at me sort of astonished.

"Well, I'm not going into boarding. If you put me into boarding, I'm going to run away. Just watch."

For a second I thought about jumping overboard.

We puttered along for a bit, not looking at each other. Finally, taking a deep breath, he said, "I'm sorry if you think I've been a bad father."

"So am I."

Boom.

I remember once, a couple of years before, him and my brother were having some hassle about the boat, about putting out the bumpers before nightfall. And Harper was holding out, saying, yeah fine, but they're not always necessary, depends on the weather. And the old man was getting more and more pissed off, not because he was right but because he was getting contradicted, and he took a couple of steps toward Harper like he was going to hit him; only Harper just stood there, eyeball to eyeball with the old man, he was daring him, their chests just about touching, me just about having a stroke from all the excitement, and there was that moment when the old man just stopped, he knew he couldn't push it any farther, there was nothing left to do now except hit Harper and if he did, there was a pretty good chance Harper was going to kick his ass all over the living room. He made a face, like he had something really bad-tasting in his mouth. And I remember thinking, Hmm, this is a new ball game.

He started to wind in his line. You could hear the click-click of the big reel, drops of water quivering on the line until the lure came dancing along the surface. He pushed the throttle slowly forward. The hull rose up and then planed and we headed for home. On the opposite shore, I could see the dock at Tally-Ho Inn where I caught a five-pound bass once. The waves went plink-plink against the hull and I found myself thinking about that Physics exam when I lay out on the grass and I imagined a day like this.

Just as we were pulling up to the dock, he said, "Do you really mean that, Simon? That I'm a bad father?"

It was like a splinter I'd stuck in him and I was the only person who could take it out. I didn't answer. But not because I was a fucking sadist, but because I could feel it slipping away from me, that sense of being absolutely right, and I was starting to feel like a heel. But I didn't want to let him off the hook.

We got out of the boat and clunked the stuff on the dock and I was thinking to myself, God, I should say something, take it back; but it didn't seem quite right so I thought, I'll do it in a minute. And then we were walking through the swamp and I thought, when we get up into the field I'll say something; but then we got to the field and he was walking a little bit ahead of me so I thought I'd wait till he slowed down. If he slows down, I thought, it means he wants me to say it and I will. But he didn't and then we were at the foot of the hill, the house above us and we started up, but it's quite a strenuous climb, not the sort of situation where you want to spit something out, being half out of breath and all, and then we got to the top of the hill and just as I was about to pop it, we saw the old lady sitting in a deckchair on the back lawn and she waved to us and the minute she waved, it was like the fishing trip was over, we weren't alone any more, it was like a stranger had just sat down at our table and now we were both trying to be on good behaviour.

We went down a little dip in the field and up onto the lawn.

"So," my mother said, "how are my favourite boys?"

I walked past her into the house and went into the kitchen. I was pouring myself a glass of orange juice when he came in. He took the ice tray out of the fridge and then came over and stood beside me. I shot a look over at him, he was cracking the ice but he was waiting for me, his face sort of open and expectant, like he was going to say something nice if I just gave him a chance. But I didn't. I didn't have the nerve any more. It was gone.

Next morning he went back to the city. I lay upstairs waiting for him to come up and say goodbye to me. I was going to say it then. But he didn't. He just loaded up the car and took off.

CHAPTER SIX

A WEEK LATER I ran into Greg's younger sister, Margot, at Hidden Valley. She was fourteen, skinny and not that good-looking but weirdly sexy. I mean there was something about her that just gave you an instant boner. She came out to my cottage once wearing a little turquoise two-piece bathing suit and I kept looking down her halter top. We ended up playing some stupid water game with a bunch of kids but I got Margot on my shoulders, those bony little knees on each side of my head and I'm telling you, it was all I could do not to give her a good *bite*.

Anyway, she was having a cigarette out on the balcony and we started talking and after awhile we went for a walk over to the mini-putt. It turned out she was going off to camp in a few days. She was a junior counsellor at Camp Skugog. You could just imagine her tucking those little kids in at night and then going back and singing songs by the campfire, all the guy coun-sellors waiting for everybody to go to bed so they could be alone with her. Maybe I have an overactive imagination but you get the picture.

We ended up sitting on a hill overlooking the chalet where the dance was happening. It was a warm night and the grass was soft and there was kind of a magical feel to everything, the band starting up, and after awhile Margot lay back in the grass and looked up at the stars and said, "What would you do if this were your last day on earth?"

"I don't know," I said, "what would you do?"

"I better not tell you. It'd freak you out."

She put her hands behind her head.

For a second there, I could hardly get my breath.

"No, I'm fine, tell me."

"I'd probably go to bed with somebody. You don't want to die without ever having done it. But you've probably already done it."

She looked over at me, my head going sort of pins and needles. I had a feeling she was waiting for me to kiss her but I didn't want to get it wrong and have her screaming bloody murder up on that hill and calling for the police and everyone knowing I was a child molester.

I lay down beside her, staring up at the stars like I gave a shit, and casually I sort of rested my arm against hers. She didn't move it. I touched her hand. I could feel her fingers move just a little. I sat up and pretended to stretch and looked over at her and then I leaned over and brushed her cheek with my fingers.

"What?' she said.

"You have a little grass on your cheek."

"Oh," she said, looking right at me. "Did you get it?"

I leaned down and kissed her. She had a nice mouth, all wet and warm, and next thing you know we were rolling around on the grass, me rubbing my hips against hers until I found myself moving toward that dark planet again. And then everything went completely white and it was like some devil had left me. I'll tell you though, for a young girl, she was certainly experienced. Afterwards, she asked me if she could have a look and she unzipped my shorts and lowered my underwear and just kind of stared at my dink, sort of doodling and then smelling her finger. Jesus.

We went back down the hill and into the chalet. I talked to everyone. Really, I felt like a movie star. I can't remember ever feeling so smart, like I could do nothing wrong.

When I got home I told Harper about it. He got sort of a pained look on his face, like I'd done a bad thing, but I had a feeling it was something else. Like when a guy is getting too much luck. It's cool at first but after awhile you wish he'd fall down a mine shaft or something. Or at least keep his fucking mouth shut. Which is very hard to do. I mean one of the great things about girls is talking to other guys about them. And to be honest with you, I didn't feel bad at all, I thought the whole thing was a gas, especially that bit with smelling her finger, except when I imagined Scarlet hearing about it, that moment when someone hears something terrible and their face goes kind of blank. So I decided to spare her. Just write it off as another bad thing I'd done that no one needed to know about.

Somewhere near the beginning of August, there was a phone call. The old lady took it, talked for a bit and then came out to the backyard where we were shooting arrows into this cardboard box.

"Boys," she said, holding a cigarette down by her side, "we have to go back to the city tomorrow."

"Fantastic," I shouted, "who died?"

She gave me a dirty look.

"We have to get up with the birds and I don't want to have a big fight. So get your stuff ready tonight, okay?"

When she went back inside, Harper whispered, "Must be the old man."

Next morning, around noon, we headed down to the city.

It was a beautiful day, everything just gleaming the way it does when you're happy. Harper sat up front with the old lady, talking about this and that. I sat in the back, reading magazines and looking out the window. It's a boring drive, I've done it like a thousand times, I know all the boring rocks and little restaurants beside the road, the gun store, the bridge, the turnoff to Bracebridge, that long deadly stretch of rolling hills and then nothing to look at between Barrie and the city. It went pretty quickly but still, by the time we rolled down our street, the houses nice and close to each other now, it felt like a different day from the one we'd started back at the cottage.

I raced in the front door, my mother hollering after me to take something in first. I went up to the maid's room and I called Scarlet. Like I thought I was going to have a fit if her line was busy or she was out. But she was there.

"I'm back," I said.

"When are you coming over?"

"When should I?"

"Tonight," she said. "And hurry. I've got something to show you."

That was all I needed. I blasted back down the stairs, taking them two at a time, and went out to the car.

"Nice try," Harper said.

"Boys," Mother said in her warning voice. Travelling made her a little jumpy. She just wanted to get in the house, have a noggin and put up her feet.

I loved being back in town. I loved the way my room smelled, that moment when you first open the door and go in. I got a whole lot of stuff out of my drawer, a kilt pin from an old girlfriend, a love letter from Daphne Gunn on blue tissue paper (actually she never looked like a potato till she dropped me), a Searchers 45, a broken transistor radio, and laid it all out on the bed. But I got used to it pretty quickly and stuffed it back in my drawer without looking at half of it.

That night I went over to see Scarlet. It was one of those great nights in the city where you feel like something is calling you outside. I mean you can just about hear these voices, "Come out, come out." I headed up Forest Hill Road. I didn't get a half a block before I broke into a trot. I don't think I'd ever been so happy before, all this stuff to look forward to, Scarlet, being back in the city, the way the air smelt, all the lights flickering in the windows, the cars going by. It was like more than my body could keep inside. I was talking out loud to myself, trying to explain to my imaginary audience just how amazing it was, like it wasn't enough to just think it, I had to actually say it, find the exact right words. I cut down through a little park where I used to go tobogganing with Kenny Withers, and then turned left on Chaplin Crescent. You could smell the rose bushes. That's some kind of flower. Like a drug or something. One sniff makes you feel like you're not living up to scratch, you should be having a better time. But this one night down on Chaplin Crescent, for once I wasn't waiting for my life to start. For once I had a life as good as the one you imagine when you smell roses.

I figured it must be her father who came to the door. He was a tall, gangly guy with a moustache, wearing a pair of white cream slacks and an expensive shirt. But here's the weirdness. His hair was brushed down over his forehead in a Beatle haircut. Very strange on a guy like that. I tried not to look at it. I mean apart from the hair he was a pretty classy-looking guy, sort of like Errol Flynn.

"And who might you be?" he asked.

"Simon," I said. "Simon Albright. I'm a friend of Scarlet's."

"Ah yes, Scarlet," he said, crossing his arms like he was trying to remember the last time he saw her. I had the distinct impression he was fucking around with me.

"And what time were you going to see your friend Scarlet?"

"Nine o'clock."

"What time is it now?"

"Nine o'clock?"

"It is quarter past nine. Have you no timepiece?"

He waited for a second and then burst out laughing.

"Come in, come in," he said. "I'm just playing the fool."

"It's nice to meet you, Mr Duke," I said.

In the living room was a plump woman in a red dress and a bald guy I'd seen before somewhere.

"I'm Barry," the mophead said. " And this is my wife Sherry. And I'm sure you know Elwy."

That's where I'd seen him. The bald guy had some TV show where they showed old black and white films and interviewed people nobody gave a shit about any more. You know, like a cameraman on some 1940s movie. For some reason I pretended not to recognize him. Just so he wouldn't think I was a groupie. But he seemed like a pleasant enough guy, old Elwy, beaming away at me. Some people just like new faces and I guess he was one of them.

"Sit down. Please. Emily will be right out," the woman said in a British accent.

Emily?

For a second I thought I was in the fucking twilight zone. You know, guy goes to wrong house and picks up wrong girlfriend and nobody notices.

"Emily," she called. "Emily."

I heard Scarlet's voice coming from the bathroom.

"Christ! What!"

"Your friend's here."

"Well tell him to wait."

Then the door shut again.

"Well-spoken girl," I said, and looked around the room for smiles. Nothing.

"So where do you stand on all of this, Simon?" Barry said. He was leaning forward in his chair with a big green goblet in his hands, one of those glasses you use in a castle or something and I suddenly realized he was pissed.

"All of what?" I asked.

"On this business of breaking the law."

"I don't think he has the faintest idea what you're talking about," said Elwy, who gave me a wink. I think everybody was too pissed for him and he wanted me to know it.

"I mean where do you stand on this business of breaking the law?" Barry went on, as if I'd tried to ignore him the first time. "Some people say everybody breaks it. Other people believe it's a sacred trust. I say the law's the law and you bloody well should obey it. What about you?"

"Depends on the law," I said.

"What's that supposed to mean?"

"Like, I don't feel it's my inalienable right to go around dropping blasting caps in people's mouths while they sleep."

He frowned.

"It's a joke, Barry," the woman said.

"But you think it's all right to break *some* laws," he said. "Do I understand you correctly?"

"Yes. For sure."

"Like what?"

"Well, let me see. When do I think it's all right to break the law? When I jaywalk, for instance. When there's nobody coming, I don't lose a single night's sleep after I jaywalk."

"So you think *you* have the right to decide which laws are worthy of respect."

"Well . . ."

"Don't you think that's rather pompous? Just imagine if everyone went around doing that. Making up the law as they go. Then where'd we be?"

"But I'm not everyone," I said.

"Meaning that you're smarter than anyone else. What grade are you in?"

"Grade Twelve."

"And you think having a Grade Twelve education entitles you to break the law? That's a bloody irresponsible attitude, I'd think."

"But Barry," his wife said, "you break the law all the time. You speed on the highway. That's breaking the law."

"Well that's how I feel and I'm bloody well not going to apologize for it. Right, Simon? Simon understands." And then he kind of pushed himself back into his chair as if we were begging him to say more, but no, no, that was enough, thank you very much. I had that slight fluttering in my chest and my hands were sweating like they do when I feel like I'm under attack. Somehow you always come out of those conversations feeling in the wrong.

"What movie are you going to tonight?" Elwy asked me.

"*Mondo Dante*," I said.

"Oh dear," he said and gave me another wink.

"That's one of our films, isn't it?" the woman added.

"I'm afraid so," Elwy answered and sort of winced, like

somebody was about to smack him with a newspaper. I looked over at Barry. He was sitting peering down into his glass.

Scarlet came into the living room, wearing dark eye make-up. Sometimes girls look so pretty they're sort of scary. I could smell the vanilla across the room.

"Oh, there you are," said her father.

"We should be going," Scarlet said. She was wearing black shorts and a white T-shirt.

"Tell me this, Simon," Barry said. "I suppose you think we should legalize prostitution. That'd be just fine with you, wouldn't it?"

"Daddy!"

"Well, wouldn't it?"

"I honestly don't know, Mr Duke. I've never thought about it."

"That's not the only thing you haven't given much thought to. Do you honestly think Grade Ten will prepare you for this life?"

"Well Mr Duke, I wasn't planning to . . ."

"Rubbish! Come off it, mate. Grow up! Get out there and bang on some doors."

"Which doors?" I asked.

"Just bring her back intact, that's all I say," he roared.

"Barry!" his wife said.

Elwy winced again.

"Where are you going, by the way?" Barry said.

"They're going to a film, dear."

"Which film?"

By now I was moving very quickly toward the door.

"*Mondo Dante*," I said.

"That's ours, isn't it?" Barry said.

"Jesus," I whispered.

But he jumped into action. He went over to the coffee table and snatched up the phone, his hair still hanging over his forehead like a fucking moat boy.

"Hello?" he said, "this is Barry Duke at Universal Pictures. I need a couple of passes for tonight's show."

He grinned, and raised his finger quickly in the air to silence me. Then the smile fell off his face.

"Duke," he said. "Barry Duke."

"Oh-oh, somebody's going to get in heck," Scarlet said, sitting on the arm of a chair.

"*Duke*," he repeated slowly, getting pissed off. "D-U-K-E."

By which time I was about ready to leap out of the window. He put his hand over the mouthpiece.

"Clueless," he said. "I've told them a hundred times. *Hire nationals*!"

"She's probably new," Sherry whispered. "At least she speaks *some* English."

"Done!" Barry said, slamming down the phone.

"Well *done*, dear."

"Somebody was almost out of a job," Scarlet said.

"Really, Mr Duke, I didn't mean to pick a fight here. That was just a joke about the blasting caps."

"So I keep hearing. But it's no joking matter, if you ask me. Given the way things are going."

"Oh for heaven's sake, Barry, *what* things?" his wife said.

"Just read the newspaper. You'll see."

We opened the door and I was stepping out when he hollered, "Don't hate me. I'm testing your mettle, that's all. Be grateful it's coming from a friend. Bloody idiots! Don't stand up for anything any more."

Out in the corridor, the door shut, Scarlet said, "He's going to have a terrible hangover in the morning."

"I should hope so," I said. "My goodness."

"Don't take it personally. He just likes to argue. He thinks it makes people think."

"About what?"

"I don't think he liked that remark about the blasting caps. I heard from the bathroom. I think he thought you were making fun of him."

"I was."

"Well, you shouldn't. It's very hurtful to have someone your age make fun of you. Particularly in front of everybody."

She walked on to the elevator.

"Did *you* think I was rude?" I asked.

She took a breath as if she was losing interest in the subject.

"No, just a bit superior. But that can really set somebody off. You thought I was making it up didn't you?" she said.

"What?"

"That he was a big shot."

"No," I said, "I didn't."

"He can get tickets to anything."

"I'll bet. Who's Emily, by the way?" I said.

"Oh, that's just a pet name. Only my family calls me that. Everybody else knows me as Scarlet."

"What name's on your birth certificate?"

"I don't know. Emily probably. What's it matter? I like Scarlet better. Come on," she said. "This is getting off on the wrong foot."

So we went down in the elevator. But I was rattled. I mean when people don't like me, I usually figure it's my fault, I've done something to provoke it. Been too mouthy or something.

And I'm usually right. Anyway, it's stupid but I sort of wanted to go back to Scarlet's place, go in, be funny, say something really clever, get everybody to like me, including her father, and then split. That way I could enjoy the evening.

But it was too late, we had to go to the fucking movie.

We went to the Imperial down near Dundas Street. It was this grand old place with red plush seats and a high domed ceiling. There were tickets waiting for us at the window. A woman with a white cone hairdo gave them to us. She seemed kind of neutral to me, but Scarlet didn't see it that way.

"See what I mean?" she whispered, "she doesn't want any *more* trouble."

We sat beside the aisle. The lights went down. Scarlet threw her legs over the seat in front, and rested her hands in her crotch.

Sometime during the movie, I felt her staring at me and for a second I had a feeling she was trying to figure out if I was good-looking or not. I don't love the way I look from the side. I don't have very memorable features and I have a soft chin, I know that, it's a nice face more than a handsome one, so I don't like people staring at me for long. Finally she went back to looking at the movie but she didn't say anything, which was unnerving. I mean you'd think if she was thinking something good it would have just burbled out on its own. It worried me. Thinking bad things about the person you're with is just the worst kind of loneliness.

"What did you want to show me?" I whispered.

"I'll tell you later," she said, not even bothering looking over.

After the movie was finished, we came out onto the street.

"Well, that was a complete and absolute gross-out," I said.

"Yeah?"

"Like it left me feeling I was covered in cobwebs."

"I liked it."

"You did not. You couldn't. Nobody could."

"Speak for yourself."

"All those midgets and perverts and creepoids. God, where did they *find* those critters?"

"You're so judgmental. They're just people, Simon."

"Not from my neighbourhood, they're not. God, it's enough to make you believe in compulsory euthanasia."

"What's that?"

"Mercy killing."

She took one of those deep breaths you take when you're trying not to let somebody bug you. "I liked the theme song, too."

"Yeah, that was all right. What was it called?"

"How should I know?"

"So what do you want to do now?"

"Beats me. I'm sort of pooped actually."

"You want to go home?"

"Might as well. Nothing going on down here."

"Why would your father be interested in a movie like that?" I asked after a minute.

"Because it makes money, Simon. Duh."

By the time we got to the intersection, I'd had enough. So I just said it. "Scarlet, do you not *like* me any more. Is that it?"

"No, I'm fine," she said.

"Well I'm not. I have the feeling you've been looking at me all night like I'm something a pigeon left on your parents' balcony."

She broke out laughing.

"Jesus, Simon." She walked on a bit and then stopped.

"God, it's the strangest thing. It just broke right through everything," she said.

"What did?"

"Oh God, that must mean I like you again. Don't hate me for this, all right? Don't. But I was really looking forward to seeing you. Like *too much*, you know? And then when I saw you in the living room, it was sort of a disappointment. I imagined that you looked different or something. And I thought, Oh God, I don't like him any more. And then you said that stupid pigeon thing, and it was so *you*, and I thought, Oh God, I *do* like him after all. It was like we just connected, the second you said that."

"So you do like me?"

"I just told you. Yes."

"For awhile, I have to tell you, I sort of figured things were kaputskyville."

"Well, now you know. Now we both do."

"So what did you want to show me?" I said.

"Never mind. It's stupid now."

"No, tell me."

"My tan," she said. "Don't you think I'm brown?"

After that it was easy, and sort of unimaginable how all the weirdness had happened. It was Scarlet again, instead of this super-cold bitch who was thinking the very worst, very truest things about me.

We walked up Yonge Street, all lit up and bustling on Saturday night, and turned west along Bloor toward the Village. It was jammed, busloads of tourists driving through; tough guys on motorcycles, skinny girls with their hair parted down the middle. Some of them smelt like incense, you could smell it when they walked past you. A go-go girl danced high in the second floor window of the Mynah Bird. We stuck our noses into a basement club across the street; there were four guys playing in the band, pretty cool-looking, with their long straight hair cut like the Kinks and those Edwardian jackets.

"*It's your life*," they sang, "*And you can do what you want.*"

The drummer doing a slow roll around his drums, ending up on the floor tom and giving the high hat a whack with his stick. Then they all came in:

It's your life
And you can do what you want.
But please don't keep me waiting.
Please don't keep me waiting . . .

Very cool. An unimaginably cool life. Just the sound of the cymbals hissing and the electric guitars booming out onto the street made me ill with excitement and envy. The drummer was a kid my age and I got that weird, anxious feeling again, like I was never going to have a life as exciting as that. That I'd already missed the boat.

We came back out on the street. Some asshole tried to sell me some poetry. I'd seen this dickweed in action before. Eric the Poet. Bucktoothed, glasses with fishbowl lenses, he was about the ugliest son of a bitch you ever laid eyes on. But people liked him, they thought he was the real article, you know, a real live bohemian selling his wares in the street. Sometimes they'd invite him to sit at their table in an outdoor café and after a minute or two he'd be wailing away at them, telling them what bourgeois, brainless assholes they were and they'd sit there like children, sucking it in, thinking they were having a real experience. Unbelievable. I mean that fucking place, Yorkville, it was a great big fat fucking fraud. You could just feel it.

I ran into a friend of mine, Tony Osbourne, who'd dropped out of school. There he was with no shoes on, long hair, and living with a beautiful girl over top of the poster store. I used to like him, he had some magical way of getting older guys to let him hang around with them. But he'd gone sort of cool on me since he'd quit school. Like I was a square who didn't see the big picture. But his girlfriend sure was a dish; long black hair, bony little hips in tight jeans, you just wanted to reach down and bring your hand up right between her legs. Honest.

We stood there shooting the shit outside the poster shop, putting it on a bit for the chicks, me trying to get it across that I had some pretty wild friends and him, well, God knows what he was up to, maybe just out and out amazement that an asshole like me had such a classy girlfriend.

Anyway, after awhile the chicks started to get restless, they sort of knew what was going on, and we moved along. When we got to the corner, Scarlet said, "I like your friend Tony. He's sort of mysterious."

"Yeah, well, we'll see how mysterious he is when he's living in a cardboard box, selling pencils."

"In today's society," she said, "you've got to make room for everybody."

I don't mean to be a snob, but when somebody starts a sentence with, "In today's society," you don't have to listen to the rest of the sentence. Even when it comes out of your girlfriend's mouth. Funny thing is, it was sort of reassuring to hear Scarlet say something stupid. It made her less scary.

We started up Avenue Road and I caught a glimpse of the big round clock at the top of the hill. The Upper Canada College tower. For a second I thought it was the moon.

"So what do you want to do now?" Scarlet said.

"Beats me."

"We could go back to my place. They'll be asleep by now. My father gets up at five in the morning. Reads the trades."

The trades. Very polished, very adult that. We were silent for awhile and I found myself wondering if she was smart or whether she just had a good memory. Collected neat stuff she'd heard and then just spouted it. Like *Reads the trades*.

We caught the bus at St Clair, the one that goes up through Forest Hill. It was always empty, that bus, lit up and flying down those quiet streets. The air smelled different in this part of town. We got off near Dunvegan Road and went into a little circular park. From there you could hear the city below. Her head leaned a little against my shoulder, I touched the side of her face with my hand, I moved my head down very slowly, I could hear her say something. Then I kissed her.

"Come on," she said, and she pulled me off the bench. "Let's go back to my place."

Quite frankly I sort of hoped her old man would still be up, maybe we could have a decent conversation and end this all on a good note, but the old guy had just had too many noggins I guess, and he was sawing logs somewhere in that big white apartment.

"Do you want a drink?" she asked.

"Sure."

She disappeared out of the bedroom and turned up a minute later with these big green glasses on a tray. I could hear ice cubes clinking around inside.

I took one of the glasses and peered down into it and took a sniff. It made me shudder.

"Jesus Christ, Scarlet," I whispered, "what's this?"

"Scotch and coke. It's the Beatles' favourite drink."

I looked at it again.

"Don't analyze it, Simon. Just drink it."

"Are you sure the Beatles drink this stuff?"

"Positive."

She sat on the side of the bed, holding her elbow, this big green glass in her hand.

"You don't really drink, do you?"

"Not motor oil."

In a little while, she put her glass down.

"It's too bright in here," she said and put a red scarf over the lampshade.

"Is this going to be all right?" I whispered.

"As long as we're quiet."

We lay down on her bed. In a sort of mechanical way, we started smooching, as if, you know, it being the end of the evening and us being boyfriend and girlfriend, this was the sort of stuff we were supposed to do. But when I lifted her shirt up, when I looked down her body, at the dip from her ribs to her tummy, I could feel something black stir in me.

She was on top of me, sort of kissing me, then lifting her head back and looking at me, then kissing me again. It's not my favourite way of kissing, it makes me vaguely self-conscious. From that angle nobody's very attractive. But she kept doing it, slowly lowering her head, touching her lips to mine. They were dry, she'd been smoking. Suddenly she threw back her head and then smashed her teeth down on my lips really hard, so hard she cut me. I mean I could actually taste blood in my mouth.

"Jesus, Scarlet," I said, sitting up, "what the fuck is going on here? Like are you mental or what?"

She was looking at me, all still, as if she was waiting for something. I wondered if maybe she wasn't a bit bonkers.

Sometimes when I was alone, walking along the street or staring out the window, I found myself rehearsing conversations with the old man. I hadn't seen him since the blow-up in the boat but I knew I was going to and I kept thinking about what I was going to say. But, even in my imagination, it always seemed to go badly. I'd start out the conversation with some line I liked, but his answer, the one *I* gave him anyway, always seemed to find the chink, the essential chink, in my armour and I'd be back at square one. On top of which I wasn't pissed off at him enough any more. Over the weeks I'd sort of slunk back to being scared of him. Except when I thought about boarding. When I thought about that, it was like so shameful, so embarrassing to be put in there, like your parents checking you into a leper colony, that I'd get hot all over again. Find myself talking out loud to him on the street. Sometimes I imagined him hitting me and me hitting him back. Sometimes I even imagined me socking him first. Man, that would have surprised the shit out of him. Pow!

Anyway, one day we went up to see him. It was Sunday, natch, shitty things always happen on Sunday. I sat in the back of the car and as we got up near the city limits, I spent my time picking out really crappy apartment buildings and imagining I lived there.

Mother went in to see the old man first, *comme fucking d'habitude*, and then Harper. Meanwhile I wandered around the halls, getting extremely uptight, imagining all sorts of things. I saw that daffy old broad again; she was clanking around the halls, smoking a cigarette, talking to everybody. Finally I went in, he was lying there on his bed, looking pretty fucking feeble I've got to tell you. Soon as I saw him I was sort of relieved. He was a lot scarier in my imagination.

"How are you?" I said.

"I'm fine. Hope it wasn't too much damned trouble, coming on a Sunday."

"No," I said. "How's it going up here?"

"Getting bloody tired of it."

He looked over toward the window. "Have you given any thought to what we talked about?"

"Which part?"

"Don't be facetious," he said.

"Mother said it wasn't for sure. She said you were just putting the house on the market to see what you could get for it."

"Did she?" he said, like everybody was fucking up on him and it didn't even surprise him any more.

"I was sort of hoping that held some water."

"Yes, well we want to see if *you* hold any water."

For a second I felt it, like everything was happening very close to my face. Like all I had to do was push it away. Fuck him, I thought, I don't have to listen to this prick any more. What's he going to do? Get out of bed and chase me down the hall? I was getting ready to walk out. I just needed one more provocation.

"What do you mean by that?" I said.

But it was like the old man could hear me thinking, like he could feel the moment build up and up and up, like those cicadas in the fields just before they go dead quiet.

"Nothing," he said, like he was letting go of a rope. He looked out the window and I suddenly had the mind-blowing idea that that I was *stronger* than he was now. I mean, physically.

"I'm not going into boarding," I said.

But the second I said it, it seemed like I'd taken one step too far. Now I was just being a prick and I felt weirdly unprotected. Like somebody was going to cuff me back into my place.

The way he looked at me, you could tell he hated me. Like if he could have pushed a button and exterminated me, he would have. A million times I remembered him giving me that look and me just shitting in my pants. *Oh-oh, I'm in trouble now.* But now it just set me off.

"You know," I said, "if I thought we were just going to get up to our usual bullshit, I wouldn't have bothered coming."

He made that face again, like he had a piece of rotting fish in his mouth. "You're a real gent, Simon," he said. I was just about to answer when suddenly I saw his eyes water up. I'd never seen that before.

"Damn treatment," he said, wiping them quickly. "Get your mother for me, will you?"

I stood there for a second, not sure what the hell to do.

"Go get her, please, Simon."

That *please, Simon* went right through me. I mean I could feel it. It was like a fucking dagger right in my heart.

I went out in the hall.

The old lady went in.

"What's with the old man?" I said to Harper, who was standing with his arms crossed, leaning against the wall.

"They zapped him," he said, putting an index finger to each temple. "Maybe it'll make him less of an asshole."

I looked at him blankly.

"They put electrodes on the side of your head and then they plug you into the wall."

"What do they do that for?"

A nurse in a green smock passed. He watched her walk down the hall. "Makes you less depressed."

I squinted at him.

"No shit," he said.

"They plug you into the wall?"

"Yeah. Just like a vacuum cleaner. Or a toaster."

"Sure thing."

He shook his head. "It's true. Like dropping a bag of marbles on the floor."

"What is?"

"Your brains."

CHAPTER SEVEN

W<small>E WENT BACK TO THE COTTAGE</small> but it was starting to get boring up there. I was lying around the
house and getting in quarrels with my brother; even
school was starting to look good. Finally the old lady had had
enough.

"God's teeth!" she declared one afternoon, "what's *gives*?
Why don't you go down to the city for awhile?"

So I went to stay at my Aunt Jean's house. She was the wife
of my drunk, dead uncle who croaked on the living room
couch, six in the morning. A sad story that but anyway. She
lived in a big brownstone house on Poplar Plains, this narrow,
windey street that runs from downtown up to my neighbourhood. Her son was sort of weird, a gun nut, a hunter and a
member of some religious cult. After he hit puberty, we never
really got along. He scared me a bit, not that there was anything
hostile about him. He was just sort of long and pale and creepy.
Anyway, they'd shipped him off for the summer to work on a
shrimp boat on the west coast and his room was empty. So that's
where I went.

I liked my aunt, she was nice, and I liked staying at her
house. I'd get up late, just before noon (it was the middle of
August now), and perch my chin on the windowsill while I was

waking up, peer out onto the street and watch the cars climb slowly up the hill. She left me lunch in the kitchen, a tuna sandwich and a cookie and a glass of milk, all laid out nicely, like I was still a kid. But that was fine. We didn't know each other very well. She worked as a volunteer somewhere over by Eglinton with the St John Ambulance people. Organized book sales and auctions, things like that. She was a little lonely I think.

Anyway, I'd go downstairs and eat my sandwich and watch TV and just hang around the house. Sometimes I'd listen to the Beatles on her stereo. I could turn it up real loud. There was a song I liked, "It's Only Love," a slow, mushy one and it had this part in it when the guy's voice goes way up and it gave me goosebumps.

I used to play that part over and over again in that big empty house. There wasn't much else to do, most of my friends were still away at their cottages.

Some evenings, when it was just getting dark, I'd go to the front door and open it and just stand there, this soft sad summer street, no one around, all the colours kind of muted. There'd be these lights twinkling in the windows, I could smell the lake, the stars winking over top, the wind in the trees, the leaves making that funny swishing sound and some nights it made me very sentimental.

Sometimes I'd go for a walk barefoot around the neighbourhood just so I could feel the stones under my feet, the hot pavement. The grass. I was hungry to feel the sensation of things touching me. Sometimes it was just so *much* that I felt like having a cigarette. Something to bring it down a little.

Near eleven at night I'd head down to the fairgrounds to the Exhibition. That's where Scarlet worked. It was down by the lake and I'd walk to the foot of Poplar Plains and then go over to Bathurst and catch a streetcar. I'd sit near the back, looking at my reflection in the glass and we'd rattle on downtown. Off in the distance you could see the rides, the ferris wheel whirring backwards. And I'd know Scarlet was down there and that soon I was going to see her. And one night sitting in that streetcar, I tried to imagine not having her to go to, I thought to myself, one night you're going to be sitting in a streetcar and you won't have Scarlet to go to. And really, I couldn't imagine anything more terrible. What would I do? Where would I go? How would I spend my time? What would be worth doing? I'd be like a little grey man walking around in a circle.

And then the streetcar'd get down to the lake shore and rattle around a corner and head along the shore, the bell clanging and we'd get out, a whole crowd of us, everyone all Saturday-night excited and pass under the great big gates with the angel on top, thousands of people on a summer night. And I'd push my way through them, head over through the midway. You could hear the balloons banging and the whistles whistling and the bumpity cars crashing into each other and pretty girls screaming on the roller-coaster, air rifles going pop, pop, man, it was like the whole world was down there, it was like the centre of the universe, all lit up and everyone there. I'd pass through the midway and nip up the stairs of this great big mausoleum, the Food Building. Inside there was free food and people looking at cars and boats and guys with their dates and I'd hurry down the aisles and over near the back of this huge, wide open floor, there'd be Scarlet. She'd be standing on a little round stage, still as a statue. All dressed up in fancy clothes, people standing around watching her. She'd stand like that for a half hour, not moving, nothing, just her eyes closing every so often. And then suddenly, like magic, her arms'd come to life, all graceful, they'd rise up and hang there for a second, and then settle on her hips, and then her face'd come to life, she'd smile, there'd be a little round of applause. And she'd go to the side of the stage and down a little set of stairs and come over to me. And people would look at her and then at me and then we'd leave together. And you felt like everyone in the place thought what a lucky fellow I was.

We usually walked back through the midway, played a dart game or got some ice cream at a stand. One night we got our picture taken, the two of us squeezed into a booth. That picture makes me a little queasy now.

And then we'd catch the streetcar back to her apartment. Her parents were always asleep and we went into her room and shut the door and fooled around. We went a little farther than before but she still kept grabbing my hand and pulling it out of her pants.

"Don't," she said.

"Why not?"

"Because."

"Because why?"

"It's not right, right now."

One night, I got quite pissed off and sat up.

"You've done it before," I said. "Why won't you do it with me?"

"Well, I haven't really."

"You said you did."

"Well not all the way."

"What do you mean?"

"Well, he got it in just a bit."

"Well, why can't I get it in just a bit?"

It went on like this for a couple more nights. Finally she gave in.

"All right," she said. "But not tonight."

"Well when then?"

She thought for a minute.

"Next Monday. That's my day off."

"It's not going to take all day."

"Look," she said, getting pissed off, "do you want to do it or not?"

"Yes," I said.

"Then it's next Monday. I don't want to be rushed."

So we set it up like a dentist appointment. That's how it seemed to me. Except I didn't argue. I didn't want her to change her mind.

"And don't forget to bring a rubber," she said, which didn't sound very romantic. I just nodded.

And then I went back to my place, up the stairs through my aunt's house. There was a note reminding me I was supposed to go shopping for school clothes with my dad some time. I got into bed, I lay there with my hands behind my head. The ceiling was very low in my cousin's room, it being on the third floor. On the other side was a cupboard with a brown wooden door. I had opened it earlier, the first day I was there, but there was something about it I didn't like, something sinister. It might have been the smell of someone else's clothes, I didn't know. But I figured I owed myself a peek in there, just to make it less spooky. I wondered if there was a light in the cupboard. I could have got up and checked but it was easier to see if I could remember. I moved around inside the cupboard until I got sleepy. Then it didn't matter if there was a light; I'd wait till tomorrow or the next day to have a look. There was plenty of time.

On Monday, near two o'clock in the afternoon, I was sitting in the window on the third floor, looking down on the street when I saw Scarlet making her way toward me. She was

wearing a yellow dress. I yelled out her name. She stood looking around.

"Up here," I said. She came and stood under the window.

"Hi," I said.

She made a face.

"Nice day eh?"

"So far," she said.

She disappeared under the windowsill. The doorbell rang. It
was one of those old-fashioned ones, made this irritating buzz. I
heard my aunt's voice way downstairs. I always liked the way
Scarlet talked to grown-ups. She was so sure of herself, sunny
and all. Some kids are good at sports, some kids are good at math;
Scarlet was good with parents. She stayed down there awhile
shooting the breeze, being charming and knowing it. Basking in
my aunt's approval like a cat in the sunshine.

Finally she made her way up the stairs, holding onto the ban-
nister. I stood at the top, sort of posed. Somewhere in the house
there was a radio playing, it was always on, it kept my aunt company and at this particular moment the newscaster was rhyming
off the traffic accidents over the weekend. Nine dead and four
injured.

"Here's one more," Scarlet said deadpan as she went into the
bedroom. She looked around. Went over and sat on the edge of
the bed. I sat down beside her and put my arm around her and
gave her a little pat on the back, like something you'd do to a
kid whose cat had just been run over by a car. Not very sexy.
Not really a mood setter, if you know what I mean. And then
gradually I moved my face around until I found her lips. But it
was all a bit mechanical.

"Can I have a cigarette?" she said. I pulled back.

"Don't be mad. I've just got to relax. I'm nervous."

She fumbled around in her purse and brought out a gold pack. Very chic, the cigarettes long and thin with a black filter. She lit it with a man's lighter.

"Where'd you get the lighter?" I said.

"My dad. He gives them out to all the film execs."

"You'd think they could afford their own lighters."

"Can I have an ashtray?"

I went downstairs and got her one. I ran into my aunt in the kitchen. She was flapping around down there, making something.

"Scarlet is so nice," she said in a whisper. "Really, you should marry her."

When I came back, my future wife was sitting on the windowsill, as far from the bed as she could get. I was trying not to let it all piss me off because, truth is, I wasn't really in the mood either. But I sure wanted to get it over with so that down the road, when anyone ever asked me, had I done it, I could say yes and not feel all fluttery-stomached like you do when you're telling a whopper. I could just look him right in the eye and say, casual as dropping a penny in your pocket, sure. Besides which I'd spent so many nights daydreaming about just this moment that now that it was here and nothing was happening it seemed like an extra piss-off.

"It's too light in here, " I said. Something I should have realized earlier, the sunlight streaming through the window like the Fourth of July, no wonder no one could get in the mood. I needed something to cover the window with. But there were no curtains except for these teeny tiny little white things that looked like something you tuck in your shirt if you're eating muffins. So I got off the bed and went over to the mysterious cupboard. I opened it up. Jackets, shoes, funny-coloured shirts

I'd never wear. But up on the top shelf, there was something red, folded neatly. I pulled it down and it came unravelled on the floor.

"Wow," I said. "Look at this."

Scarlet leaned on her elbow. "Just what kind of a cousin is this guy?"

It was a flag, big as a bedspread, blood-red with a big black swastika dead centre.

"Looks like the real thing," I said.

"Can I have another cigarette?"

"Jesus, Scarlet. Do you want to do this or not?"

"Sure," she said. "I was just asking, that's all."

"Well, you're not making things very easy."

I took the flag over to the window and pinned it there with a couple of tacks I'd popped out of a calendar. It worked all right, casting a dark, red shadow over everything. Like something out of *Murders in the Rue Morgue*.

Suddenly, like she just remembered she had a bus to catch, Scarlet stood up and came over to the bed and pushed me back and lay on top of me. She tasted like cigarettes and I liked that. It tasted foreign and exotic and grown up. She was kissing me on the mouth and pulling her head back and I was afraid she was going to do that thing again so I rolled on my side and suddenly it got very sexy, just the angle or something, her mouth all warm, my eyes closed, the side of her face all wet and nice smelling.

In a little while Scarlet sat up and lifted her yellow dress up over her head and took off her undies. I had to sort of wrestle around with the rubber, my hands were shaking, I couldn't get it to roll down right, it was upside down, and then I couldn't find the right spot. But then suddenly I was inside her. And it felt like my real home, like the only place I should ever be. I moved back and forth and I was thinking to myself, how do I know how to move like this, like how do I know this is the right thing to do? And then I had a sensation like all the nerves in my body were combed backwards, it just washed right over me again and covered me in goosebumps.

She didn't knock. She just came straight in with a tray of peanut butter sandwiches, pushing open the door with the toe of her shoe. But when my aunt got a gander at that red room with the Nazi flag over the window, she beat it out of there in reverse like someone had jerked her with a rope.

Scarlet didn't waste any time. She flew out of the bed, walked into her shoes and went downstairs, still fiddling with a hook at the back of her dress. Next thing I hear, standing at the top of the stairs, my eyes out on sticks, is the two of them talking, not about anything, just talking, Scarlet chatting away like nothing at all had happened and my aunt going along with it. I tell you, she was some cool customer, that Scarlet. Like a cucumber.

We ran into my aunt on the way out, everybody bending over backwards to avoid everybody, and we had a little chat about dinner, me just about hysterical with politeness.

"Can I get anything at the store?" I asked, which was pretty unusual for me.

"No," said my aunt, "I think we're fine, dear."

That was as close as we ever got to talking about "it."

A few days later, I got up late. My aunt was out. I went downstairs and had my toast. I put on the Beatles and I went to the front door and looked up and down the street. I was feeling a little weird, I don't know why. Maybe sleeping too late; you can gas yourself that way, after awhile the body stops throwing off the carbon monoxide and you start poisoning yourself; having all sorts of bad dreams. I couldn't remember any of them but they weren't good and it was a relief for my eyes to pop open and realize that none of that stuff was true.

I started back up the stairs, the Beatles in the background, and I noticed a little stain on the carpet, near the bottom. It just stuck in my head and I had that feeling again, that, for no particular reason, I was going to remember it forever.

When I got up to my room, I was fooling around in the cupboard, looking for something to wear when I noticed that Scarlet had left her sweater there. I knew she'd be looking for it, I made a mental note to tell her and then I forgot about it like immediately. The cupboard didn't smell so weird anymore; didn't seem so alien. But I had a feeling maybe there'd be something else nasty in there, hidden way at the back, skin books or a gun, something like that, but I didn't have time to look today. I felt strangely rushed, as if I ought to be somewhere, like I'd forgotten something, left a door open or the stove on.

I walked downtown, following Poplar Plains until it hit Davenport and then Davenport over to Avenue Road. It's a depressing intersection, lonely and grey and everything too far apart, it's like nothing interesting could ever happen there. It always makes me uncomfortable that corner, like it's telling me something bad about my future, that I'm going to end up a bum there on a Sunday morning if I don't do things right. I don't know *what* things though. My homework and not bragging, I guess. I headed down Avenue Road and everything got better immediately; the stores were close together, people wandering, a Chinese lady with an armful of flowers, a couple of pretty girls in shorts. One of them smiled at me. Then, in front of the Place Pigalle, I ran into a guy from school. He wasn't really a friend but I hadn't seen him for a long time and so I'd forgotten the things I didn't like about him. I rather fancied the idea of telling him about Scarlet, if only I could find a way of bringing it up without being too obvious.

"Let's see if we can get served," he said. We went into the Pigalle, down a set of stairs and into a dark room. Real stinky and stale, like they hadn't opened a window down there since the nineteenth century. It was a college bar, quite famous actually, but since school was still almost a month away, there weren't many people there. We sat near the back in the darkest part of the bar, these frosted fish-eyed lights on the wall. A guy in a vest and a white shirt came over.

"A couple of draft," my friend said. He said it so coolly, it sounded so professional the guy just went and got them. He didn't ask for ID, nothing. So we sat there shooting the shit and ordering more beers and I found myself liking this guy more and more until we were telling each other the most personal stuff, who we liked at school, what we'd thought of each other at first, I even told him why I didn't invite him to my party. Something told me not to but it just came out and he seemed sort of interested. This big smile on his face, his lips pressed together, sort of a concerned look on his face like you were saying something important.

I was having a good time, everything sort of dense and colourful and always moving, it was a good feeling and I wanted to keep it going so I had another beer. I'm not a great drinker, I mean I like getting drunk but I don't really fancy the taste so I plugged my nose with my fingers and drained the draught right down my throat, the bubbles making my eyes water and, sometimes, I let go of my nose too fast and I got a whiff of the beer coming back up after it landed and it sent a kind of shiver of disgust through me. But that turned to gold too. I could feel it on my skin, like goosebumps, everything interesting and always moving toward something even more interesting. And suddenly I was alone, my friend had gone and I was sitting next to a big table of kids, they were university students and I hoped they would talk to me and finally some kid did and I got into a long conversation with him, his friends on each side listening at first and then going back to their conversation. We got to talking about everything under the sun, politics, Vietnam, stuff I don't normally get into, not really knowing anything about it. But I got quite animated, even argumentative about something, I can't remember what and then the guy turned back to his table and I was alone again. I put my feet on the chair in front of me, this big jar of beer sitting on the table and I started squinting my left eye, I don't know why, I was trying to see if I could do just one eye at a time but the guy in the vest came over and told me it was time to move along. I could see the people at the other table were sort of listening but none of them came to my rescue, not even the guy I'd had the long talk about Vietnam with, so, feeling kind of like I was in a movie, that an audience was watching me, I got to my feet and ambled very slowly toward the door.

By the time I got outside, it was getting dark, a single star sitting in the sky, the sky a sad blue getting darker toward the horizon. I took a deep breath, still thinking I was in a movie, and shuffled off down the street. I got down to Bloor, saw a man who looked like my father coming out of the Park Plaza. Had the same kind of walk, his arms slightly stiff. I put my hands in my pocket and looked around, waiting for someone to talk to me. I wandered over to Bathurst, the street a bright blur, over-hearing bits of conversation. Planning the things to tell Scarlet about my day, things I'd thought about the world on the way down there. I caught the streetcar. I slumped in a seat and down we went; the bell clanging, people walking along the sidewalk looking at us lit up inside like a goldfish bowl. Like a travelling goldfish bowl, that's what we were like. Then I was walking under the Princes Gates, they were lit up like crazy, the sky dark now, stars out, the Wild Mouse whizzing around high up; I watched the roller-coaster creep like a big bug up the side of the rampart. It hung there for a second, right at the very top; and then this kid in a white T-shirt raised his arm like a battle charge and then whoosh, down it came, rattling like mad, girls screaming.

A man dressed in a lima-green panda suit waddled through the crowd.

"Who's that there inside that suit?" I said, grabbing him by the arm but he pulled away and kept going.

I was just bouncing up the stairs into the Food Building when I saw Scarlet at the top of the stairs. I let out a holler and went up and threw my arms around her. She was with one of her friends, a skinny girl in a red sweater. I'd met her before.

"Hi, Rachel," I said, "Still talking about yourself?"

Scarlet made a face and looked over at her friend.

"Nice guy," she said. It was true though. Last time I'd seen Rachel, she couldn't stop talking about herself, no matter what the subject was. But I figured she'd have at least have a sense of humour about it, like I had about being drunk, but apparently not. She kind of looked at Scarlet.

"I don't get it," she said.

"I'm just joking," I said. "How are you?"

"You've been drinking," Scarlet said.

"All day," I said.

"See you, Scarlet," her friend said. "Bye, Simon."

"Bye-bye, Rachel," I said. "I was just kidding about you talking about yourself all the time."

"That's okay," she said, meaning it wasn't okay at all, that she was just tolerating me because she was a good sport. Last thing I remember is seeing that red sweater disappear into the crowd, her face turned around and a sort of TV commercial smile on her face, her hand raised.

"What an asshole," I said.

"Simon!"

"Well, she is. Stuck-up little twat."

That was when I saw Mitch moving across the midway; he was wearing white jeans, his hair just so, as always, and I called out to him.

"Simon!" Scarlet whispered frantic-like, but it was too late. He broke away from the crowd and came over to us.

"Hey guys," he said.

We shook hands.

"Scarlet."

"Mitch."

"So what's up?" he said.

"I've been drinking beer all day."

"Looks good on you," he said. "What about you, Scarlet?"

She told him she worked over there in that building and that loosened things up a bit. We started across the midway, the three of us, me in between. While they were talking, I slowed down a minute. Let them get closer together. I figured I was doing everyone a favour. Nothing perverted about it. I just wanted her to get over him and the sooner she stopped jumping out the window when she saw him, spent like five minutes seeing he was just a normal guy, the sooner she'd get there. In fact at one point I went over and played a dart game, leaving them to talk without feeling like I was breathing down their necks. By the time I got back to them, they were easier with each other. Scarlet was at least looking at him now.

"So what do we want to do now?" I said. You could sort of tell Mitch wanted to hang around a bit so I said, let's go over to the rides, see what was up. I liked it that everyone was friendly.

"So where's Chip?" Scarlet asked him, referring to some guy they both knew, and Mitch started to answer, saying he hadn't seen much of him this summer, not since that business at the party. What business at the party, she asked, and he started into a story about this party somebody named Strawbridge had, it was quite a long story and Scarlet thought it was pretty interesting, laughing here and there along with him, the two of them sort of on the same wavelength. After awhile I started to feel not so good, at first I didn't know what it was, the beer wearing off, that good feeling gone and a sort of hollow feeling came on and I could feel myself drifting away from them, like they were caught up in one world and I was definitely in another. And when I tried to interject, to get involved in the conversation, I had a feeling like I was butting in. So I fell silent, deliberately not talking, thinking that any second now Scarlet'd pay me some attention, ask me a question, something. I even stopped for a bit, pretending to look down at a ring-around-the-coke-bottle game, pretending to get some change from my pocket, but really to see if she'd even notice. They walked on a bit, Scarlet listening hard to this story, nodding her head, like it was important, like she was on his side, making all those agreeing noises. Then the two of them came slowly to a halt, not even looking back, like they sensed there was a reason to stop but they didn't want to break up the story. I came up quickly behind her and gave her a hug and she sort of stiffened and put her hand on my hands but she kept on listening to that fucking story.

"Come on," I said, "let's get on a ride." And I walked on ahead like I was taking charge of the situation but when I got to the ferris wheel, I turned around and they were gone. For a second I wondered if they'd given me the slip. But then they came through the crowd, talking away, quite close to each other, physically I mean, Scarlet not at all afraid of him any more. And Mitch showing no signs of having anything else to do or any intention of going anywhere.

"Come on, Scarlet," I said, "Let's go."

"I can't," she said, "I'm afraid of heights."

"Come on Mitch then," I said and as I said it I had the distinct feeling that I sounded like a loser, like I was asking for a favour, like I knew he'd say no before I even asked, the way a loser does.

"No way, man," he said.

I was starting to look very bad and it made me angry, like a hot red flash, Scarlet letting this all happen, so I sort of spun around and went over and bought a ticket and got on the ride, like I was all alone. And for sure I expected Scarlet to break away and come over and ask me what was wrong or say, hang on, I'll come, I'll come. But she didn't. It was incredible. Just fucking incredible. She sort of stood there, beside him, the two of them looking like a couple, like she was with him, and watched me sitting on the ride. I even thought they might be talking about me, like, Jesus, what's wrong with him? You know, like I was the problem, like they were *joined* by it or something.

So the attendant comes over; clicks down the safety bar and suddenly I have this feeling, like I've made a bad mistake, that I can't leave the two of them alone together, like that's what they want and I've just handed it to them on a fucking twenty-four-carat platter.

And then I see them walking over this way, they buy tickets, she gives me a big smile and then they get on the chair below me. I think, thank God that's over with. At least they're close by. Nothing can happen with me this close. The ride bumps up a notch and I rise up, the chair swinging back and forth. I turn around in my seat and say something, like, "I forgot I'm afraid of heights," which they both laugh at. Scarlet makes a face, like she's scared too, but she makes it at *him*, and it's back, the feeling that there's something between them, some kind of invisible language they've got. Like she's looking to him to be nervous with. And then we got up another notch and another couple gets on; and then another and another and I'm going up higher each time, looking down, my stomach not feeling too good at all. All the fun gone from the booze now. My hands holding onto the bar real tight because, in fact, I really *am* scared of heights. I'd never've taken this ride on my own. And all the while, I'm craning around in my seat to shout at them feeling awkward and not as funny as I was before. Sort of reaching, if you know what I mean. And then we start up, up, up we go, getting to the crest, my hands holding on like claws, really scared now, letting out a whoop, too scared to turn around in my seat, the whole city reeling out in front of me, lights and people way, way down there, hands sweating like crazy. And then down, we're plunging down, I steal a quick look over my shoulder and Scarlet's staring at her knuckles, being really scared with him, like he's looking after her and I'm over here, just as far away as the man on the moon.

Around and around and around we go, up and down we go, city lights rising and falling, rushing toward, then racing way, it goes on for an eternity, this ride, just for fucking ever. And when we finally slow down, I stop right at the top of the city, I'm rocking there, I can see all the way to Upper Canada, its big tower, the yellow clock face, it's sometime after midnight, that gets burnt into my brain.

"Whoa!" I shout and turn around very carefully in my seat. I'm not drunk now, I just feel ill and I can smell myself. But they're not with me, they're not paying attention, they're talking to each other, Scarlet holding onto the bar, her head turned toward him, Mitch listening, that hair flopped over his brow.

"Hey, you guys."

Scarlet looks up. "Hey, you," she shouts, then looks back down, like she's taken care of me, now she can get back to it. But what's *it*? We hang there a moment longer, then we click down. People are getting off below me, it's taking forever. Finally I get out of the chair and go over and pretend to talk to some old couple, like I'm a real character or something, but really I'm killing time till Mitch and Scarlet get the hell off that thing and when they do I kind of stagger over to where they are. Except no one laughs. Everyone is looking a little too serious. Like they're working up to something.

"I think that's enough for me tonight," I say, by which I mean, Mitch, go away. I want to be alone with my girlfriend now. But it's not like talking to her, it's like talking to them. Like they're sharing a brain, like they've undergone some mysterious transformation and they're the same person now.

"Yeah," she says, "well, I don't know."

And she looks over at Mitch to take her cue from him. He wanders away a few steps, and suddenly I know I'm in real danger.

"What's up?" I said, the smile on my face like cardboard coming unstuck.

"I want to be with Mitch now."

I turned slowly on my heel and walked away. I walked about a hundred yards into the midway, seeing nothing. The farther I walked the crazier I felt. It was like peeking inside a furnace. I turned around. I couldn't even see them, I stood on my tippy toes, looking here, looking there, but nothing. Then I started to make my way back through the crowd, slowly first, in a sort of thoughtful way, in case they were watching me but then faster and faster until I arrived back at the ferris wheel at a full gallop. But they were gone. I dove back into the crowd again, running from game to game, down one aisle, up the next, back to the ferris wheel, in case they were looking for me there, my heart going a zillion miles an hour, like I was in a total complete panic. But they were nowhere. Gone into thin air.

I blasted over to the streetcar stop and hopped onto one that was just shutting its doors. I sat up beside the driver. I figured if I sat there, I could hurry him up, he wouldn't dawdle if he saw me looking at my watch and throwing myself back in my seat every time we hit a red light.

Finally I got uptown. I darted off the streetcar and ran along a quiet, dark street, then another, went up a small hill, blasted along another. I was getting a stitch in my side, it was really killing me, I was running along holding my side like I'd been shot. I ran by a group of kids, they stopped talking to look at me, I kept going until I got to her place. I went into the lobby. I rang the buzzer. I didn't give a shit who I got up. Finally I heard a voice. It was her father.

"Is Scarlet there?" I said.

"No. I thought she was with you."

"Yeah, well I lost her on the way home."

"That wasn't very clever."

"But she's not there with you?"

"I already told you that."

"You're sure?"

"Have you no timepiece, Simon?"

"A what?"

"It's one o'clock in the morning."

I walked away from the speaker, back outside, my hands on my hips, breathing hard, sweat pouring down my chest, a bad taste in my mouth, it was like blood or bits of lung. Timepiece? What kind of fucked up bullshit is that? You mean like a watch?

I looked up and down Chaplin Crescent. Nothing. I went across the street and sat down in a clump of grass but I couldn't sit still. I was just too agitated and I walked over to Eglinton and then back; and then I went a bit down the street and turned around and came back and just when I got opposite her apartment building I saw the two of them come walking along the sidewalk.

I ran up to them.

"Do you mind if I speak to Scarlet for a second?" I said.

"No," Mitch said. He put his hands in the top pockets of his jeans, just like a cowboy and shuffled off down the sidewalk. I waited till he was gone and then I took a deep breath.

"I'm feeling quite weird," I said and laughed, sort of.

"Me too," she said.

"Sort of like a nightmare."

"Yeah."

"I was looking for you guys down at the Ex."

"We went back to the Food Building. I forgot something."

"Oh yeah. What?"

"Just a thing."

"Right. Did you find it?"

"Yeah, it was in the make-up room."

I shifted my balance and then slipped my hands in my pockets.

"This is pretty weird."

"Yeah."

"So what do you think?"

"I think it's sort of kaput."

"Really?"

"Yeah."

"Are you sure about this? I mean if you are that's fine, I just want to be sure."

"I think I am."

"Well, wha . . . , what happened?" Like I never stutter but I just couldn't seem to wrap my tongue around the whole word. I almost expected her to burst out laughing, might have been better if she had, really, would have meant at least she wasn't talking to me like I had two heads and came from another planet.

"I guess it was just supposed to happen."

"Can I just ask you a question?"

"Sure."

"Like what would've happened if we hadn't run into Mitch?"

"I would have called him, I guess. Sooner or later."

"Really?"

"Yeah."

"That makes me feel a little better."

"Really?" she said in a way that dropped me right down the black hole again. Like she wasn't worried about losing me at all, just that I might be all fucked up and her responsible.

"Just seems like a funny time for this to happen," I said, talking about what happened at my aunt's.

"Yeah," she said, sort of making a face, like she didn't want to think about it.

"Did you tell Mitch?"

"No."

"That's good," I said, meaning we still had a secret, something that was just us.

"Was I really the first guy?"

"Yes," she said.

"Are you sure?"

She started crying. "I really don't want to talk about this now."

"What are you crying for?"

"Because it's sad," she burst out. "It's sad, that's all."

"Yeah, well. You'll get used to it." I scuffed my foot across the sidewalk. "God, I can't believe this is happening."

She looked down the street. I waited, it was like for a death sentence.

"Well, it is," she said and wiped her eyes and then gave me a sort of brave smile like this was something terrible happening to both of us.

"You sure about this?" I said and didn't like the sound at all, like I knew I was cooked.

"Yes," she said, surer now.

"Well, I guess that's it."

She didn't answer.

"I guess I better start looking for a new girlfriend."

"You'll find one," she said and of everything that got said, that was the worst.

"I've got to go," she said.

"Why are you being so cold about this?" I said.

"I'm not. I just feel bad for Mitch."

"He'll keep."

"I just don't know anything more to say."

"Well, that's great. After what, two months?"

"I told you. I guess I'm just not over Mitch."

"Yeah, well maybe you should have . . . ," I stopped myself. I suddenly realized it didn't matter what I said. It wasn't a school debate, you can't talk somebody into liking you.

"I'm going," I said.

"All right," she said.

"Fine. So you're going up with Mitch?"

"No, Mitch is going home. He was just about to leave. I was walking him to his car."

"Did you kiss him?"

"Simon, please. Just go home."

"You did like me, didn't you, Scarlet? I mean I didn't imagine all this, did I?"

"Of course I liked you," she said and touched me on the arm, but I had the feeling she was doing it just to hurry things along.

Mitch ended up driving me back to my aunt's house in his parents' car. I talked the whole way, not about anything, just bullshit. It was like I had a black train coming up behind me and if I stopped talking, it was going to charge right over me.

Finally we got to Poplar Plains. I got out of the car.

"I'm sorry about this," he said.

Weird thing is, he was too. You could see it. On top of everything else, the prick was a decent guy.

"That's all right," I said, "I've got another girlfriend anyway," and bounced up the stairs and turned around to give him a wave. That way maybe he'd give her a good report.

But he'd already gone. He didn't see fuck-all.

I stuck the key in the lock, my hand shaking so hard I could hardly find the keyhole. I opened the door. It smelt like a museum inside. I went up to my bedroom, I took off my clothes really fast like somebody was chasing me, I washed off my face and my chest in the sink, I brushed my teeth, I looked at myself in the mirror, and then I hurried across the room in my underpants, never feeling so skinny before, and got under the covers and pulled them up and closed my eyes, tight. Wow.

The next morning when I woke up, I had a fucking anaconda wrapped around my chest. I could barely breathe. I lay there for a second, just surfacing, trying to figure out what was wrong. Then it landed like a two-hundred-pound bag of cement right on my head. I groaned out loud. Oh Christ. I tried to go back to sleep, it was way too early, just a few birds and that sharp yellow sunlight.

I've been dumped before, so I know you can tell the difference between a girl who's pissed off at you and a girl who's dumping you. I mean what scared the shit out of me with Scarlet, why I felt like dropping through the centre of the earth, was the *absoluteness* of it. You could feel it, just the way she talked to me. No wondering. No, should I? shouldn't I? Just hand me the axe and arrivederci Roma.

To make matters worse, the old man was coming by to take me clothes shopping for the new school year. One of those projects some wizard dreamed up at the loony bin, you know, get involved with stuff, and he had to pick this morning to do it.

At nine-thirty on the buzzer, honk, honk. I looked out my window and there he was. Sitting in his blue Morris, right in front of the house. Smoke putt-putting from the exhaust pipe.

I went down and got in.

"Hi," I said. "How's things?"

"Hello," he said, real brightly. He was clean-shaven but looked shaky, sort of pink the way people do right after they shave.

We drove up through the city, it was Saturday morning but, really, I'd never seen the place look so barren, so pointless. It was like some awful outskirts-of-hell place.

"Sleep well?"

"Yeah. Great," I said.

"How's your friend?"

"Who?"

"I'm sorry. I've forgotten her name."

I didn't say anything.

"It's the damn treatment."

"I don't know who you mean," I said.

"Sure you do. Your girlfriend. The model."

"Oh, Scarlet."

"Yes, Scarlet."

"She's fine."

"I hear she's lovely."

"Yes."

"She must be going back to school soon?"

"Yeah, that's right," I said, sounding sort of surprised, like the thought had just occurred to me. I almost broke into a whistle to throw him off the track.

"Everything all right there?"

"Yeah sure. Why?"

"Don't know. Just want to be sure. Want you to know that you're free to talk to me about this stuff. Any time you like."

"No, everything's peachy," I said.

Peachy?

"Look, Simon, I don't want us to get off on the wrong foot today, all right?"

"Absolutely."

"We'll get this out of the way. Then we'll have a spot of lunch."

"Terrific."

"You seem a little preoccupied."

"Who? Me?"

That day was the longest day of my whole life. We went up to Beattie's on Eglinton, a store that specialized in rich little fucks who went to private schools. Ridley, St Andrews, T.C.S., Upper Canada, even some of those Catholic schools. I kept going into the bathroom and looking at myself in the mirror. And this same horrified face kept looking back at me. *Yep, this is really happening.*

And the guy serving us. He was tall with a sort of baby lock of blond hair that fell over his forehead. He wore a grey suit with a tape measure draped over the shoulder. He wanted to know about my summer, my friends, my girlfriend. God it never stopped. I almost went insane. I had to get fitted for a jacket, for new flannels, we had to buy a whole mess of ties, a house tie, a school tie, black socks. The socks seemed especially tragic to me, harkening back to happier days when I'd jerked off into ones just like them. Now they looked up at me in a sort of accusatory fashion. Like I was going to be haunted day in and day out by Scarlet, every time I put those bloody socks on. What else? Oh, cufflinks, soccer shorts, a school sweater. On and on it went, the cash register singing away, me trying to be appreciative, trying to make the old man feel like I was glad he was there whereas in fact all I wanted to do was finish up and go hide back in my Nazi-loving bedroom. Just lie on the bed and stare at the ceiling and listen to my heart crash and wait for something to happen that I knew wasn't going to. For Scarlet to call me; she'd made a terrible mistake, she loved only me, could I forgive her?

Like I said. Forget it.

After we were finally done, the old man turned to me. "Well, what do you think? Should we get a bite to eat?"

"You know," I said, "I don't feel so hot. I think I have the flu or something. I think maybe I better go back to Aunt Jean's and just take it easy for awhile. I don't want to be sick for school."

"All right," he said, sounding a bit disappointed. "You're sure?"

"Yeah."

"We could pick up something to go."

"No, I'm fine, Dad. Really. Thanks though."

"Well, maybe today's not the day," he said.

"No, maybe not. But some other time, for sure."

He dropped me off with an armful of parcels at the door. I saw my aunt on the stairs.

"Any calls for me?"

"Not a soul," she said. "You've been abandoned."

She must have been making a joke but it seemed weirdly sinister. Why would she say that today? Did she know something? I looked down at the carpet and saw the little stain. I saw that stain yesterday, I thought. And the notion of all the things that had happened between seeing that stain yesterday and seeing it today made my stomach kind of *turn*. I was so tense, everything had that look again, like it was covered in varnish or something. Shiny and way too bright. I went up to my room and shut the door.

Sometime near midnight I went out and got a pack of cigarettes. I lay there in the dark, puffing. Fuck me.

A couple of days later, Scarlet phoned. She wanted her cardigan back. It was in the cupboard. I smelt it under the arms. It just about killed me. It really did. Then I pulled a real boner. I agreed to meet her and give it back. In person. I should have thrown it out the window. There it is, baby, come and get it. But I was trying to make a good impression, not look like a sore loser or anything, so I agreed to meet her at Eaton's right by the fountain. I got there early and then, just before she was supposed to come, my heart started fluttering like mad and I realized I'd made a terrible mistake. I was just about to sneak away when she turned up. She was wearing a brown khaki dress. Mitch was with her.

Unbelievable, eh? She actually brought Mitch. I gave her the sweater.

"Hello, Simon," she said. "This is very nice of you."

"It's all right. I was down here anyway. Had to meet a friend."

"I think I'm hung over. I finished up my job last night. My parents had a little party. You can imagine."

I saw their living room full of fabulous, sophisticated movie people. Mitch there instead of me.

"I can't stop eating. I just made Mitch buy me an ice cream cone."

Why is she telling me these things? I wondered. Nobody could say things like that, one after the other, just by accident. It's got to be on purpose.

Mitch was wearing a pair of leather shorts. They looked totally stupid. How could she like anybody wearing such stupid pants, I wondered. But that business about the ice cream, *I made Mitch buy me an ice cream cone*, like they were a steady couple or something, I just couldn't stop hearing it. It made me ill.

"I got to get kicking," I said.

Get kicking? Like where the fuck did *that* come from?

We chit-chatted for a bit longer, me feeling like my head was going to explode. And then they took off, walking real slowly, looking at this and that, no hurry at all. Unbe-fucking-lievable.

CHAPTER EIGHT

I LIKE SAYING GOODBYE to places. I would have liked to wander around our city house and say goodbye to my bedroom, goodbye to the maid's room where I spent all those hours doing my homework, goodbye to the rec room where I listened to "Little Deuce Coup," the kitchen where I spilt that pot of honey one night just before dinner, my mom walking around with this stuff sticking to her feet, waiting for me to own up.

I felt sort of guilty about those rooms, like I'd abandoned them and there was no one to look after them or think about them.

We had a circular staircase and for some reason, me being superstitious maybe, I never counted the stairs, I had a feeling it would be bad luck. So on the way up, I used to count until I almost got to the top and then I'd stop and sort of scramble my thoughts. But I always figured a day would come when it would be all right for me to know.

What really bugs me is I can't remember the last time I was there. I think it was with the old man, a few days after we went clothes shopping. I had to get a sports jacket out of my cupboard and I went up the stairs into my bedroom, the whole house neat as a pin, and got the jacket, it was herringbone, and came back down the stairs, through the hall foyer, looked at myself in the hall mirror, like I always do, and then came out the front door into the sunshine and got back in the car. But I'm not sure. Maybe I went back again. Imagine me being in that house for the last time and not saying anything, not even knowing it, just walking away breezy as a summer afternoon. Not even goodbye.

First week in September, I got stuffed into boarding school. My old man got out of the bin and him and my mom moved everything up to the cottage. All the city furniture, everything. Harper went into residence at Trinity College. Everyone just gone, poof! I mean I told those people, especially my mother, that selling the house was a bad idea, it'd fuck us up, but they thought I was just being selfish and they did it anyway. And now look. Like you didn't have to have to be Madame Rosa with her crystal ball to know that house held us all together, we were just like those fucking electrons in the physics book, you know, you take away the object they're all flying around and they just zoom off into outer space, all lost and spinning around till they just expire.

Anyway, there I was. A boarder. Me. *Quelle fucking horreur.* For years I'd been making fun of those guys, feeling sorry for them, those pale-skinned fuckweeds slumping across the quad. Now I was one of them.

My first day in residence, the housemaster, a French teacher named Psycho Schiller, took me aside after lunch and said in this slow, solemn voice, "We do *homework* on Friday nights here, Mr Albright." He said it as if he were saying, we don't have sex with animals here, Mr Albright. As if I'd somehow been morally at fault all these years going out and having a blast with my friends. But he was going to fix that now.

"In *my* house, we never lose sight of our social and academic responsiblilities," he went on to say.

Psycho loved caning boys. I think it gave him a boner. He liked to bend them over in their pyjamas, these little kids, their parents three thousand miles away, them completely at his mercy and really give them a flailing. Make them realize their *social and academic responsibilities*. Firecracker Day last year he was out prowling the quad at three o'clock in the morning, waving his cane around, just hoping to catch some kid dropping a cherry bomb out the window. What a guy!

What was even worse, I had a roommate. A fucking roommate! I'd seen this guy in the hallways before and wondered to myself, who is *that* asshole? One day last year, right after sports, I went by the boarders' locker-room, and for once they weren't jamming their pricks up each other's rear ends, they were torturing some guy, a whole lot of kids in there, chanting,

E.K.J.
Wills is an asshole.
E.K.J.
Wills is an asshole.

And throwing towels at this guy, him all hunched up in the corner, ducking and letting out these whoops, sort of digging it in a weird way, all the attention.

Well, guess what? That was my new roommate.

He wasn't a prick really. In fact he was kind of intelligent. He just didn't know how to behave, always making stupid faces or jokes that weren't funny or cheering too loudly at the football game, just no feel at all for how things ought to get done.

But since he was my roommate and there was nobody else to talk to, and him being none too fussy, I yacked at him all the time, him sitting there on the edge of the bed, with his white, white skin and little handsome head, hair always perfectly combed. He also had a remarkably big dong. Like a real monster.

First time I saw it in the showers, I could hardly take my eyes off it. It was a beast.

"E.K," I said, "how come you've got such a huge cock? Like did your mother take some weird drug when she was pregnant? It's almost like another arm."

Crack of dawn every morning, a bell went off and we hopped out of bed. Me first. I ran full speed down the hall in my towel to get to the showers. That was the only decent part of the day, standing there in the hot water, the steam rising up around me, my skin turning red like a lobster in a pot. I stayed right till the last minute, until some crater-faced prefect came in and hollered at me.

Then I had to hustle. I tore back down the hall and got dressed super fast, my shirt-tail hanging out, tie draped like a string around my neck, shirt soaked all the way through. Ran down the stairs into the quad with a whole lot of other guys, our hands in our pockets, hair wet, heading towards the dining room.

Every morning, I used to ask myself the same question: How did this happen? How the fuck did I get here? One minute I've got a girlfriend and a family and I live in a house and then I get on the ferris wheel and I go up in the sky and when I come down everything's gone; house gone, parents gone, Scarlet gone and me out here in the bright morning, my hands in my pockets, fucked.

I hadn't heard a peep from Scarlet, big surprise, eh, but by now I figured she was back in that girl's school in Quebec she was always talking about. Whose daughter went there, how the prime minister came for Sports Day. She was a real piece of work, that chick. I should have figured that earlier, though, catching her necking with that guy in my basement while her boyfriend was upstairs. Like duh, what was your first clue you're with somebody of ambiguous moral character? I should have mentioned that to old Mitch, him walking around the school like Mr Cool Balls. See how he liked that one. Like, nice girl-friend Mitch. But I knew he'd just write me off as a bad sport so I didn't even fucking look at him in school. His friends were a different story, though. I felt completely nervous when I walked by them. You know, like they all knew, they could look right inside me and see everything I was feeling like it was a room they could hang around in any time they wanted.

Thoughts like these kept me busy until I got into the dining hall. Now that was something else. Imagine a train station and you'll get some idea of the noise. Like two hundred kids schnarfing their breakfast, forks and knives and spoons clanging, prefects ordering people around, teachers up at the front table, looking bored and hungover in their shitty little sports jackets with the pads on the elbows. And the noise man, the din. Just unbelievable. You'd think it was a Roman coliseum or something.

I sat near the door, right beside Arthur Deacon who was going to be a priest and some blond kid from New Zealand who had tiny deformed ears. But because I was in Grade Twelve, a senior, ha-ha, even though they turned out my lights for me at ten o'clock on *Friday* night, I sat near the head of the table so I got second-best choice of food right after the prefects, unlike those poor little fucks at the far end, the new kids from Grade Nine, they got the leftovers, the burnt toast, the broken eggs; God they were little, those kids, I can't imagine how their mothers could have abandoned them in a place like that. Like leaving a kid in the forest. These little kids with rosy red cheeks looking just freaked right out. I was freaked out and I was like three years older.

But just when you're about to go down for the count, something always seems to happen. One day I was coming out of the breakfast hall and this English teacher, Dick Ainsworth, stopped me. He was a skinny guy in a grey suit with black hair and black-rimmed glasses, he looked like a pool shark. But he was one of those teachers who gave a shit, sitting on the edge of his desk after school talking to kids, getting them all to write poetry.

So he stopped me in the hall and said, "Albright, you look like you're going to explode this morning."

"I'll make it to lunch," I said. Which he pretended to find très clever.

"You know," he whispered, looking around like we were in danger of being overheard, "I think you've got brains to burn."

Sometimes someone does that for you; you're going down for the third time and they just reach over the side of the boat and grab you by the hair. That's what that guy, Dick Ainsworth, did that day. It just sent me *sailing*, like I was some kind of romantic character in a novel and all this had a point and it was going to be okay.

But that was the exception. Most of the time it was like being in *Lord of the Flies*, which, no shit, we were reading in English. Wild, eh? I don't think they even got it. You know, like the irony. They're always talking about the irony of this or the irony of that and then it comes along, the real thing, it just about poops on their shoes, and they miss it.

Yeah, that was some schedule we were on. Eight-thirty at night, we went for announcements, a little evening ritual where they got all seventy-five homos out of their rooms, plus me and E.K. of course, and herded us down into the dormitory basement and went over all the shit that had happened that day, you know, like we beat the Scadding House soccer team, or fucking

Andy Boyce finally got his tongue so far up Willie Orr's ass that they gave him the Latin prize and a trip to New York where, no doubt, he was going to get something really big up his own ass.

"It's a proven fact," Psycho told us one night, "that better educated people are virgins when they marry."

See what I mean? Like not only a great guy but an intellectual wizard as well. Up there in his robes, he looked like Mr Wilson, the fat guy in *Dennis the Menace*.

But then Fitz, a haunted-looking kid, came suddenly to life and whispered, "Guess who wears the pants in *his* family?" But the room picked that very moment to go silent, and Psycho heard it. He came slowly over to Fitz, raised his hands to free them from the gown and then, really quickly, bent over and smacked him on both cheeks, like he was clapping his hands, only rapid fire, saying, in time with each smack, "Fitzgerald, for two cents I'd cane your ass off."

A pricksucker of the first order, our Mr Schiller. Kind of guy you go back and visit forty years later, give him a good punch in the face for old times' sake. I know I will.

Even on Sunday they wouldn't leave you alone. Compulsory church. Unbelievable. If you haven't noticed, the theory of all boarding schools is to keep you so busy all day you don't have time to abuse yourself at night. Which shows you how much they know. Not to mention the gallons of saltpetre they poured all over our food. (I have this on very reliable authority.)

When my mother was a little squirt, my age I mean, she was sent off to school in France and they stuffed that church business down her throat three times a day. So by the time she had us she said, forget it. So I was like inches from a lifetime getaway when they got me. I guess they figured if they didn't bore me to death during the week, they'd finish me off with church.

Speaking of my mom, she called me all the time and I was a total prick to her. I'd let my voice go all low and flat and not say fuck-all, you know, just one-word answers and I knew it was making her sick with guilt but I just couldn't help myself. I really couldn't. Once I even told her I was going to kill myself, which was kind of a shitty thing to say. But I wanted to punish somebody for putting me here.

I didn't hear much from Harper but I can't blame him. We were pretty sick of each other, that happened every summer, and this being his first year in college, he had lots of stuff on the go. Frat parties and getting wrecked. Still it's funny sometimes how everyone vanishes at once, like turning on the light in the basement and all the bugs vamoose.

One night he called me from his room in residence. "Did you ever hear from that cunt, Scarlet?"

"Nope."

"That's a surprise."

"Yeah really."

"Something wrong with that bitch. Apart from having a fucked-up name."

Perceptive guy, eh? Like really putting his finger on things.

"Still thinking about her all the time?" he asked, biting into an apple. Harper had a sort of irritating habit of asking personal questions if he was getting bored with the conversation. You know, to heat things up. I don't think it ever occurred to him that it might make somebody uncomfortable.

"Nah," I said. "Fuck it." Which was not entirely the truth. Just hearing her name still gave me a jolt, like my whole body was suddenly under assault, heart pounding, sweaty underarms, and this funny sensation as if somebody had cracked an egg on my head and it was dripping down my face. *Maybe it was my brains.* 'Cause I should have known better. I mean I knew she was a fucking monster but I still thought about her all the time.

One afternoon, I was down in Forest Hill Village and I ran into that skinny girl in the red sweater, Rachel, Scarlet's pal from the Ex. I was extremely uptight, I mean I thought I was going to faint. It was like Scarlet was eavesdropping or something and I wanted her to hear that I was cool as a cuke. Next thing I knew we were having hamburgers at Fran's. I took her to the same exact booth I used to sit in with Scarlet. It was a mistake though. Soon as I sat down that Beatles song, "It's Only Love," came on over the sound system and before too long the whole thing turned into a fucking nightmare. Rachel started in with a story about her parents and how they should have got divorced but they didn't on account of her dad going to Minneapolis and getting in a car accident. I mean if there's anything worse than somebody who tells you everything that happened in some movie, like *everything*, it's someone who tells you a whole lot of stories about people you don't know. Anyway I was feeling mighty lonely sitting there listening to her go on. What's worse, she was one of those chicks that puts a curly-cue at the end of her sentences, like she's asking a question. Like, are you telling me something, baby, or are you asking me?

"So what happened with Scarlet?' she said finally. And right away I felt some fucking claw was locked on the back of my neck.

"We broke up."

"Yeah, I heard," she said. "I had a boyfriend like that once. You know everything was great but then we broke up. I think I threatened him? Some men don't like strong girls. They want to wear the pants in the family?"

I must have got a sour look on my face because she suddenly switched gears.

"I'm worried about Scarlet. Like just a few nights before she went back to school? She called me up and asked if she could stay overnight. Except she wasn't really going to stay overnight? She just wanted to tell her parents she was? It gave me a bad feeling."

"Yeah?" I said, my appetite dead as a fucking doornail, the hamburger tasting like sawdust in my mouth.

"I have a feeling she was going to spend it at Mitch's house? I had a boyfriend like that, he just wanted to do it all the time, like sometimes I'd just have to say, like, will you leave me *alone* . . ."

"You know what?" I said after a moment, just as soon as I could get my burger back on the plate, "I have to get back to the boarding house. I forgot. I'm on duty."

Just what I'd be on duty for is something she was too dumb to ask, but I hotfooted it back to the school, everything going really fast. Fortunately, it being Sunday, E.K. was out, and I just threw myself on the bed and stared at the ceiling, my head going like a frog in an egg beater.

It occurred to me, lying there, that maybe God had seen me that night on the hill with Margot, her sniffing her finger. There had to be *some* reason why this was happening to me. I mean this business with Rachel. I swear I could feel the hand of God in it. Like he'd taken time off from his other duties this fall to really stick it to me.

Late in the afternoon one day, I was walking along the fence near the south playing field, sun going down, and I was feeling sad but in a poetic kind of way. I could see myself out there, walking alone, and I kind of liked the picture. Anyway when I got back to my room I sat down at my desk and I started writing it down, all the things I felt, all the things that made me different from the other boys in the school. I put it all in a letter and I sent it to Arthur Deacon because, well, he was going into the church, he seemed like a kind guy, he never took a pat of butter before the little kids and so on. So I slipped it under his door.

Next morning, I saw Deacon on the way to French lab. He dropped his eyes like he hadn't seen me, and I thought *oh-oh*.

Maybe that day, maybe the next, I forget, fucking E.K. wandered into the room and told me he'd just heard Arthur Deacon telling some guy in the tuck shop that I was a pseudo-intellectual. But hang on. It gets worse. I didn't know what *pseudo* meant, I thought it was a *degree* of intellectual, you know like Esso Extra. I just blushed with pleasure, you know, like the word's out, I'm a brainer, everybody knows it.

So when E.K. went out again, I snuck over to his big dictionary and took a peek. And that's when I found out it's a *phoney* intellectual. Well, it was a blow. I mean I sat down on the bed, the dictionary still in my hands, and stared out the window. Just sick with it, man, just sick with it.

After that, everything pissed me off, even the smallest stuff, like a guy walking down the same aisle in the library or standing too close behind me at the tuck shop at recess. Like back the fuck off man and stop breathing all over me. Or E.K. talking to a couple of Bishop Strachan girls on the front steps one day. He was coming on like the big man on campus, a real know-it-all, and I just couldn't help myself.

"Hey E.K., is your sister still doing that trick with the donkey?" Picking on E.K, that was the bottom of the fucking barrel. But you got to be careful with guys like that, you know? I mean they seem all weak and eager to please and really fucking goofy but I've discovered that if you push them they can go off in your face like a hand grenade; it's not just rats you don't want to corner. So back in my room, E.K. came striding in like he was a prefect or something, looking dashing in a little brown suit, hair combed neat and black, glistening, and he said, get this, "If you ever do that again, I'm going to beat you to death."

Weird thing is, I knew not to smart-ass him back. He was at that nothing-to-lose place, and I flashed for a second on his body at nights getting into bed, all tense and muscular, not an ounce of fat on it. But I couldn't let it go by either.

"Do you mean philosophically or literally?"

"I mean get yourself another scaramouch," he said, sort of spitting it at me.

"What's a scaramouch?"

"It's somebody who makes people laugh."

And in that second my opinion of E.K. changed completely. It's too bad he had to scare me to make me stop fucking around with him. But that's what happened. I mean for awhile, after he stormed out of the room, I found myself talking in my head about what an asshole he was, how I'd given him a break nobody else would, how I wasn't going to be his friend any more, him snapping at me like that. Fuck him. Now he didn't even have *me* for a friend. I found myself rehearsing things to say to him, how cold I was going to be. But when he came back into the room after announcements, still giving me the silent treatment, I could feel myself coming around, wanting to make up. I can't stand tension, it makes my stomach go into a knot. So I apologized.

"Look," I said, "I'm sorry for saying that thing about the donkey, but I don't like being threatened, okay? It makes me very violent."

I think he knew I just had to get something in there, otherwise it'd look like I was scared of him. And after awhile we started to shoot the shit about the usual stuff. But it stayed with me a few days, him scaring me like that. Sometimes I just felt like bursting into tears, all the upset, and now this. Getting backed down by E.K. I mean, what's next after that? Cleaning out urinals with your tongue.

Never mind church, I hate Sundays anyway. No matter where you are, even the country, you can smell a Sunday, everything dead and still, not a fucking soul in the streets. So to keep from shooting myself, I dropped down to see Harper in residence at Trinity College. It was just the neatest place, green ivy on the walls, kids walking around the quad talking about stuff, just exactly what you have in mind when you think about going to university. I went up the stairs into the hall porter's office. He was going to give Harper a buzz but I asked him not to, I wanted to surprise him.

I didn't knock. The door was a little bit open and I stuck my head slowly around it like a giraffe. He was lying on his bed reading a book and he just about croaked when he saw me. I mean he jumped like I'd shot him.

"Jesus H. Christ," he said, "you scared the shit out of me."

I went in and sat down at the foot of the bed. We chatted for awhile about this frat house he was getting rushed for, but he started picking at a piece of dry skin on his lip, something he always did when he was worried.

"What's up?" I said.

"They invited me over there for lunch yesterday. But afterwards nobody talked to me or anything. I just hung around for awhile, feeling like an asshole, and then I split. I think I blew it. Fuck."

It was dinnertime pretty soon and he fished a black gown out of his cupboard, just like the one Psycho Schiller wears, and took me over to the dining room, this great big wooden place with a high ceiling. Some of the guys, their robes were like in tatters, it was almost a prestige thing, like who could have the most fucked-up robe and still have it qualify. I met a guy over there, a divinity student with a long face. He was a big deal in residence because he was fucking a girl who was going out with some guy who was going to be prime minister. Which, let's face it, *is* a big deal. I felt like I was talking to a celebrity, you know, very keen that he like me. I asked him all sorts of questions, which usually makes people like you. And another guy, with curly black hair, red lips, he looked like a fucking orang-utan. But he was light-bulb smart, by which I mean that sometimes you meet somebody in the world and you feel yourself in the presence of a light bulb brighter than yours. I sort of like it, really, I mean it's a little tiring, all that *reaching up*, but it sure keeps you on your toes. Best thing with those people is not to talk too much, that way you don't commit yourself. One thing about being with smart people, though, is you never want to be anywhere else.

All in all, I had a pretty good time at dinner, these guys talking about girls and God and Matthew Arnold in the same sentence. And then we did that thing where everybody goes for coffee and tea down the hall. Sort of formal and old-fashioned, but I dug it. I thought to myself, man if I went here, I'd be completely happy. I just liked the feel of the place. It was like you were in the house of God where you just knew to behave.

Anyway we went back to Harper's room. We were sitting around listening to the stereo when the divinity guy came by. He started rolling a joint.

"I don't know," Harper said, sort of frowning.

"Hey," I said. "I'm a big boy."

So we lit up a big joint. First time ever. Smoke drifting around the room, smelling like hay. Course to tell you the truth, nothing happened. I mean like we smoked the whole thing, right down to burning my fingers and then I sat back, the other two going pretty quiet on me, so much so I was reluctant to speak.

"Like am I supposed to feel anything yet?" I asked.

At which the divinity student laughed. But they didn't have a whole lot to say.

So I stared at the candle flame and waited for something to happen. And nothing did. So since it looked like nobody was going to say fuck-all and nobody was going to get up and do fuck-all either, I stretched out in my chair, my head going about two hundred miles a minute, and rubbed my eyeballs. You rub your eyeballs and some pretty wild geometric stuff starts happening, like exploding triangles and pentangles coming out of other pentangles and I thought to myself, boy, somebody should invent a camera that would project this stuff onto a screen because there's no way I'm going to be able to *describe* this to anybody. Which I was about to comment on when I started thinking about something else. Problem is, no matter what I thought about, it always ended up sort of a bummer, like it always landed on the wrong foot. Like I was thinking about our summer cottage. I was thinking about Sandy Hunter walking along the street that first day we drove through Huntsville, this pretty girl at the side of the road, her blond hair moving just a bit in the wind. And then I started to miss it, like miss that very moment of me and my mom and Harper driving through town, like it was gone forever, like I could never have it back again. And it hurt me so much, I mean I could feel it, like a sinking in my stomach. Quite involuntarily I let out a groan.

"What is it?" Harper said.

"Nothing," I said and then I moved onto some other stuff. But it didn't matter where I went that night, it always hurt me, and after awhile I sat up in this room full of fucking zombies and said, "I have to split."

There was this kind of stoned laughter from across the room. I got to my feet, which took a long time indeed, and then I got to the door, which took about a summer and half too.

Harper walked me downstairs to the main door. We shook hands, which was a bit solemn but seemed like the right thing to do. And then I was out in the night air, the stars very bright over my head, going up through Philosophers' Walk. I just walked and walked, I had this terrible ache in my heart, it was like I was so unhappy I could just burst. Everything seemed so sad and everything I'd ever done had fucked up and I just felt like I was a tiny, squeaking mouse in a big cold house.

I walked up onto Bloor Street and I went west, under the high walls of Varsity Stadium, university kids bouncing along the sidewalk toward me, all noisy and scary and extremely insensitive. Me hoping that some pretty girl would come along, she would see in my eyes all the wonderful things I am, she would just *know*. And she'd take me to a cottage in the woods, a small wooden cottage with a stone chimney where she lived with her father and I'd go inside, you could smell the wood burning in the fireplace, and I'd sit down by the fire and I'd be warm and safe forever and ever.

Instead of which I suddenly realized I was famished. It was like I hadn't eaten for fucking days. I was so hungry, so desperate for a hamburger that my heart just leapt with excitement when I realized I had enough money to get one. I hurried across the street into Harvey's. There was a guy in front of me wearing one of those team baseball jackets. Had his girlfriend with him. A real hairdresser. Teased hair, fuzzy blue sweater. Excellent at a drive-in with her jeans around her ankles but you don't want her writing your law boards. Anyway I was too fucking hungry to wait my turn so I sort of threw my order over this guy's shoulder just as he got to the counter.

"A cheeseburger and a glass of milk!" I hollered.

Nothing happened for a second, but then the guy turned around with an expression on his face like he'd just stepped in a dog turd.

"Fuck you," he said. And waited for me to say something back.

"I'm sorry," I said, "I didn't notice you there."

A bit feeble, I know, but better than a punch in the mouth, which was just around the corner.

He stared at me for a second longer, just to be sure I got the message, and then cooled it. But I'll tell you, it rattled me good. Made me feel sort of sordid, like I'd done something really bad, worse, like I *was* somebody really bad, some kind of creep covered in dog poo and spider webs. I mean that was the thing about that night, after I smoked that shit. It felt like everything I'd ever done in my life was like completely insane, like some guy going across a checkerboard and every other fucking square except the one he's on is just nuts. Like how could I have been such an asshole for so many years? Jesus, it was too much. I ended up back at the dorm holding my head, rocking myself back and forth, just wanting the whole fucking thing to stop.

CHAPTER NINE

THANKSGIVING I went up north to the cottage. You could feel the snow in the air, the leaves had fallen off the trees, summer looked like it was never coming back. There was a strawberry bush out back all bare and shivering in the wind. It was really something.

I got the same cab driver I had that time I came home from Scarlet's. That sort of set me off because I burst into tears when I got in the front door of the house. My mother put her arms around me and I sobbed away, bubbles coming out of my mouth like I was a little baby.

"I'm going to kill myself," I said, "I'm going to take a big piece of glass and cut my throat with it, I am," which was definitely not a cool thing to say to my mother, things being what they were.

"Promise me," she said, sitting me down at the kitchen table and looking right into my eyes, even holding my chin to be sure I looked at her, "Promise me that if you ever even think of doing something like that, you'll call me. Promise me."

"I will," I said.

"No, promise. Cross your heart. Let me see you."

"I will," I said, sort of weary and worried that I'd upset her. I mean she had her own problems up there with the old man, who stayed in the living room, by the way, reading a book.

So we sat around in the kitchen and talked about Scarlet. Sometimes I felt really good, like all the poison was gone from my body and I'd say, "I feel a lot better now," and my mother sort of smiled, but carefully like she was holding onto something, and about twenty minutes later I'd start feeling shitty again. It was like dirty water seeping back into the tub. And then I'd start all over again, going around and around in my head until I thought I'd turn into butter just like those tigers I read about when I was a kid.

Once I went for a walk down by the ravine, all the grass grey and flattened. I went down to our little creek, I stood there for a moment looking down into the water thinking about Scarlet, thinking about her coming back to me and when I did, I felt this gust of exhilaration. It just went straight up through me.

That night when I went to bed, I lay there for a long time in my room, the blue one with the cowboys on the wall, listening to the floors crack and squirrels and mice running around behind the walls. It was like a great big living thing, this house. And then the furnace went on. You could hear it go click and then it was like the whole place was breathing, breathing and looking after me. When I was little my mother never wanted me to go to sleep unhappy, even if we'd had a fight, and sometimes, even behind my father's back, she'd creep up into my room and give me a kiss and tuck me in. Which is what she did that night. I rolled over and looked at her in the dark. She stroked my face.

"My darling," she said, "if there was only something I could do. Something to help you."

She looked at me for a moment.

"I love you so much," she said. "I love you so much it scares me."

I took the train back to school on Monday night. I was in the compartment alone. Opposite me was a photograph but for a long time I didn't notice it. I was kind of wandering around in my head as if there was a problem I could solve, if I just looked at it the right way. But it was the same old maze, same old rat track and I never got anywhere new. Scarlet was gone, that's as far as my thinking ever got me.

Anyway, you know how you can look at something without seeing it? I was thinking about that time when Scarlet stood on her tippy-toes and her shirt came out. I should have kissed her stomach, I thought, I should have done more with Scarlet, kissed her more, felt her up more. I mean I thought she was going to be around forever, so there was no hurry. If I had her now, boy the stuff I'd do to her.

So there I was, wandering around in never-never land when the fog cleared and I found myself still staring eye level at this photograph. It was a picture of a beach with a yellow hotel way in the background. And something about it, the feel I guess, reminded me of that time when I went on a holiday to St Petersburg with my mother. We rented a house by the sea. Tall grass, sand dunes, sea gulls flying around overhead and there's a picture of me, I don't know who took it, I'm out on the beach and I'm feeding the seagulls, there's a whole bunch of them around me, one just taking a piece of bread out of my hand and I'm kind of laughing and cowering all at the same time, my mother in the background, lying on a deck chair, sunglasses on, her shirt tied at the waist. And looking at that picture, it made me miss those times so much it was like the bottom of my stomach fell out. I was just aching for it all, to be back there, the sun on my head, feeding the gulls. And it seemed like such a long, long time ago, sort of cruel that it was all *so gone*. And I thought to myself, if I can just get back there, back to that beach and stand out there again in the sand, I'll be happy. I can have it all back again. And then it occurred to me that I could, that I could run away and go all the way down there. I could do it on my own. Just like that night when I came down to see Scarlet. And just thinking about it filled me with this sort of strange excitement. It gave me something to look forward to, something to stop me thinking about Scarlet the whole time.

By the time I got back to my dormitory that night, I knew what I was going to do.

"You know what?" I said to E.K.

He was reading in his bed, propping that small perfect head on his hand while he flipped through a *Life* magazine.

"What?" he said, not looking up. E.K. was getting used to me by now.

"I'm going to run away."

"Where are you going to go?"

"Texas."

I knew they'd shake him down when I left and he'd tell. That way I'd throw them off my trail.

"What are you going to do down there?" he asked, all casual, still flipping through his magazine.

"I'm going to get some family that's lost a kid and get them to adopt me."

"You're going to get in a lot of shit."

"I don't care."

"Easy to say now. They'll probably expel you."

"I don't care. I'm leaving first."

I have to admit, the notion of getting expelled slowed me down a bit. But I thought of that picture again, of me out there on the beach under that hot sun, and it sent tingles through my body.

"When are you going to go?" he asked.

"Soon," I said, all mysterious. "Soon."

So for the next three days, I walked around school with my big secret. It was like having a ball of sunshine in my head. Nothing mattered because I was leaving.

I had a problem in my chemistry class. Only got half a project done before the teacher, a tall, well-dressed queer, Mr Bonnyman, told me to hand it in.

"It's not quite done, sir." I said

"Hand it in now or you get zero."

I thought for a second about that beach way down in Florida and a sort of smile came quite involuntarily over my face.

"I'll take the zero, sir."

That sure turned some heads, me sitting in the back, pretending not to notice, not wanting to further provoke the teacher, just doodling in my book, my insides just sparkling with sunshine, like it was bouncing off water.

I went down to announcements, Pyscho down there, going on about something, how to improve ourselves no doubt, this from a guy who stayed away exactly four years after he graduated and ran back here fast as he could. Guy'd crawl up his mother's ass if she'd let him back in, all dressed up in his black gown, like he's a don at a real English university, me thinking, none of this matters any more, doesn't matter what this guy thinks of me, I'm free of it all.

And then it was time. I just knew it. I waited until ten o'clock, until lights out, I even got in bed. I lay there for awhile, and then when the place got real silent, I threw back the covers and turned on the bedside light.

"You going?" E.K. said, propped up on his hand again, naked shoulders with freckles, and white, white skin. Hair neatly combed. He combed it before he got into bed.

"Yeah."

I pulled my suitcase from under the bed and started whipping things into it. All sorts of things, shirts, socks, two hairbrushes, two sports jackets, cufflinks, a school tie, three pairs of shoes, I mean just bullshit, I'd never been away from home, even my bronze broad-jumping medal, and then when the thing was fatter than a corned beef sandwich, Dick Ainsworth, the junior house master, walked in.

"What are you doing, Albright?" he said, looking at the suitcase.

"Unpacking," I said.

He thought about that for a bit.

"From what?"

"Thanksgiving, sir."

"Can't it wait till morning?"

"Absolutely," I said and took a shirt out and put it back in my drawer.

"Everything all right here, E.K.?" he said.

"Yes, sir."

"Nothing to report?"

"No, sir."

"Had a nice chat with your mom on the weekend. Very nice woman."

"Yes, sir."

"All right, Albright?"

"Yes, sir," I said.

"Goodnight, gentlemen."

Then he went out again. I stood there, vibrating like a fucking piano string while I heard his footsteps go down the corridor.

"Jesus Christ," E.K. whispered, face all scrunched up.

"Don't sweat," I said. I sat on the edge of the bed for maybe twenty more minutes, listening. Nothing. I could feel E.K. watching me with his bright little mouse eyes.

I packed up the suitcase, stuffed to busting with books and toothpaste, and deodorant, like I was going to be dining with the Queen in the foreseeable future. Sat on it and heaved it off the bed. It weighed a fucking ton.

I went over to the window and opened it up. The fall air went right to my head, all jewels and cold, it just blew through the room. I lowered my suitcase out the window and dropped it on the flagstones. I pulled back into the room.

"All right," I said.

E.K. sat up and pulled out an envelope from his drawer,

"Since you're really going, here. It's eleven bucks. If you stay away three days, you can keep it."

He shook my hand.

And then I slipped out the window. I landed on the cobblestones and stood still as a statue, the wind blowing around the quad, leaves rustling, this song in my head. I waited, looking around, waiting for something to move. There was no one around, not a soul, just the leaves whisking across the flagstones, so I picked up my suitcase and followed the wall under the dorm windows, ducking my head down, slipping under the big iron gate and then, seeing that the parking lot was lit up like the fucking Berlin Wall, I kept pressed right against the brick until I hit a patch of shadow and then bolted to the back gate, suitcase banging my knee. I ran down a back street. Suddenly the noise from Avenue Road, the traffic whizzing around the school, died away. I was completely alone, my heart beating like mad, this stupid song going through my head at a hundred miles an hour.

Five foot two
Eyes are blue
Koochie, koochie
Koochie Koo.

I had to put the suitcase down, it was wedging a hole in my hand. I could barely open my fist. I put it behind a hedge. Looked up and down the street. Across from me, in a big, ivy-covered house, I could see a woman in a yellow dress moving around in the living room. It looked very cosy in there like my house in Forest Hill, and I went over and knocked on the door. The woman opened up.

I put on my best manner.

"Excuse me. I was wondering if I could use your phone to call a taxi?"

She didn't look sure about that at all so I stepped back a few paces from the door.

"Or perhaps you could call one for me and I'll wait out here."

"Why didn't you call a cab from where you were?" she asked.

I hadn't thought of that one.

"Well, I did. But the driver turned up drunk, so I got out."

"The cab driver was drunk?"

"Yes ma'am."

Good little boy scout me. Like, boy-oh-boy, I'm sure not going to have anything to do with a drunk driver. Like wow, what an asshole!

"All right," she said and opened the door.

You know that great smell some people have in their foyers, I don't know whether it's that stuff they put in the bowl, the dead flowers, or perfume rubbed off on the coats or some kind of fancy wallpaper, but it always gets me. Like Pears soap. You just smell it and you imagine some kind of great life.

The woman had white hair and was a bit stout but she reminded me of my mother, sort of dignified and chatty at the same time. She was having a drink, looked like a gin and tonic to me. Just like the old lady. I tell you, that generation. Take away their noggins, they'll just like wither away.

She put on her reading glasses, the neat kind you look over top of, and I could see she had quite a handsome face, with a sharp nose and smart eyes and I figured as a girl, my age, she must have been hot stuff. I also had the funniest feeling that she was lonely, that she sort of liked having company, an excuse to open up the door and let someone in.

"Where are you going?" she asked.

I have a hard time keeping my mouth shut, even at the most obvious times, but there was something about this woman that made me want to tell her everything. But a little alarm bell sounded in my head. It was extra hard, I mean really difficult, worse than having someone not know you're good at something you are good at. I also had a feeling she might have run away some time herself, married for love, given up a huge inheritance like my mom did once (the husband before my dad). But I sat on it. Keeping my mouth shut sort of hurt me physically. I could feel it in my chest, this thing wanting to get out.

"Downtown," I said. I think if she'd pushed me, I'd have said the bus station, she'd have said, where are you going, and out it would have come. But she didn't. Maybe she figured it wasn't polite to ask a stranger so many questions.

She dialled the number and ordered the cab and we sat there for a bit, me looking around and telling her I liked the house, telling her it reminded me of my old house over on Forest Hill Road.

"What happened to your house?" she asked.

"They sold it."

"That must have been hard."

"Big mistake," I said. "It was a big mistake."

"Well, I'm sure they had their reasons."

I was getting awful close to telling her, I just *knew* I could trust her.

"There's your cab," she said and then I was sure of it, that she was sad to see me go. That big, empty, beautiful-smelling house and just her.

She opened the front door.

"You should put a coat on," she said. "It's not summer any more." She rubbed her arm and sort of bent over and looked down the street.

"You can say that again."

She shut the door behind me and I went down the walk. Just as I got to the hedge, I looked over my shoulder. She was peeking at me through the window and gave me a wave. I waved back. You know that time I came down to see Scarlet? When I left the next morning, I was walking down the hall and I got to the elevator and I looked around to see if she was still there. But she'd gone back inside. I didn't want to make a big deal of it, I wanted to leave on a good note but I had the feeling just for a split second, that if she had really, really liked me, she'd still have been there. I've always had that feeling. I guess I should have known right then. Not that it made any difference. No, I'd have liked Scarlet no matter what.

Well anyway, that's over with, I thought, and got in the taxi.

The bus station in Toronto is not a place you'd take a girl you liked. I mean it's sort of beat up and depressing. I know I sound like an asshole saying this but it's full of poor people sitting around, luggage tied up with strings and stuff busting out of cardboard boxes, they're smoking cigarettes and dropping the butts on the floor. Gruesome. You just can't imagine these people going anywhere nice, just some shitty little town up north where they'll sit around in some too bright kitchen and smoke cigarettes and have nothing to say to the person they're visiting five minutes after they've arrived. I know this is true because up in our cottage we have a party line and sometimes in the summer, I used to pick up the phone real gently and wrap the mouthpiece in a tea towel so they couldn't hear me breathing and I'd listen to the phone calls, country people, and they never used to have fuck-all to say to each other, these big silences, and then one'd say, well, I guess I better get the washing done and then there'd be this big pause, and then some woman on the other end'd say, "Yep," and nobody would do fuck-all, not hang up or anything, just sort of sit there, this big silence and I'd think, fuck me. Don't believe that shit you hear about country people being just like the greatest human beings on earth. Because it's bullshit; they've got the slowest, most boring lives you can imagine.

Anyway the bus station was full of these people, some guy even had a transistor radio playing country music, that stuff where the guy sings out of his nose, real shit-on-the-boots stuff. I hauled that fucking suitcase over to a bench, the place blue with cigarette smoke, and I went over to the ticket counter.

"Can I have a ticket to Buffalo?" I said, figuring Buffalo was the closest American city.

"Round-trip?"

"Just one way."

The guy looked at me, I couldn't tell why. "You got some ID?" he said.

"Yep."

"You'll need it at the border. That's five dollars and twenty five cents. Bus loads over there in an hour."

Figuring the cops might be looking for me already, like maybe E.K. blew the whistle on me, and if they were, the bus station'd be the first place they came, I hauled that two-ton suitcase out back of the bus station, found a shadowy place under a wall across the street and just stood there, watching the cars drive by. The prostitutes standing on the street corner. The sad old men going up and talking to them. Jesus, I don't want to end up like that, I thought. Standing there, I just couldn't figure out how so many people had such shitty lives. Like why didn't they just run away like me. Go south to Florida. Get a tan. Start all over again.

Anyway.

There I was, watching for the cop cars., I mean that's the thing about growing up in a place like Forest Hill. Going to school in a place like Upper Canada. I mean you have this feeling, they give it to you early on, that there's this great big fly swatter hanging over your head, it's always there, just hovering, and if you fuck up, it's going to come down on you, wham, just like on those poor fucking deer flies in the garage. Just wham. And that'll be the end of you. Like that poor Philip Foster who got expelled for burning down the Centennial tree. I saw him marching across the quad that last morning, head down, people looking at him like he was on the way to his execution. It scared you just looking at him, thinking, that could be me, that could be me, thank God it ain't, and making a big promise to yourself that you were going to mend your ways, do your homework, stop talking in class, never take a drink till you were legal. And where did he go, this kid who got expelled? I never saw him again, it was like he fell off the edge of the world.

It was scary, all that, the notion of getting heaved out, of not belonging any more. Sundays in the spring, twice a year we had a church parade, got all dressed up in our blue horsehair uniforms and rifles and berets and gaiters and polished buttons and belts and marched down Church Street, the drum core banging and slamming away, the sound echoing off the buildings, crowds of people standing on the sidewalk watching, us feeling like we were the crème de la fucking crème, seeing these raggedy-ass kids pointing at us, making fun, pretending to march, and me thinking all the time that they were jealous, that they wished they could go to a school like that, where they dressed you up like soldiers and marched you around for the whole world to look at, four hundred kids marching down the street in time. All belonging. Belonging to something. You had the feeling that if you took a wrong step anywhere, down came the fly swatter and next thing you knew you were standing by the side of the road with a dirty face watching these kids walk by. Thinking, God what assholes, but secretly wishing you were one.

All bullshit. All scaredy-cat bullshit.

So I stood out there in the shadows and I saw a big silver bus pull off Bay Street, rocking back and forth, coming around the corner, and pull into the train station. I could hear the doors wheeze open. I knew that was the bus. I waited till the folks got out and then I hurried over. Just the driver was there.

"This the bus for Buffalo?" I said.

"Twenty minutes."

"Can I get on board?"

I climbed onto the bus, leaving my suitcase by the luggage compartment. I went right to the back. The windows were dyed sort of green. I slipped into a seat. Funny thing is, with only a little while to go, that's when I started to get really nervous, like here I was, just minutes from a clean getaway. A cop car pulled into the station. Waited there a minute, just like a sulking dog, you know, doesn't know whether to steal your garbage or bite someone, and then, yellow lights going on, it moved, really slowly, down the ramp and down onto the street.

I got so nervous I wanted a cigarette. I jumped down and went into the variety store next door. A Chinese guy was working at the counter. I asked for a pack of DuMaurier's, the kind my mother smoked, paid the guy forty-five cents, got some matches and ran back to the bus. I was in such a hurry I could hardly get the tin foil off the pack. I lit up, took a big puff, the smoke rolled out of my mouth, this blue cloud and the smell of the tobacco reminded me of the old lady, when we used to go for those drives in the country at night, and she'd ask me to light one up for her.

"God's teeth," she'd say, "I hope I'm not making you into a smoker."

People started getting on board.. They seemed friendly enough, I didn't want to make any enemies, so I helped a guy with baggy jeans hanging around his ass put a parcel up in the overhead. A girl with a blond pony-tail and dark eye make-up came down the aisle, sort of snobby, like she was afraid someone was going to try and pick her up and was telling them to fuck off ahead of time. I could smell her perfume. I had a feeling she'd just finished screwing her boyfriend, and I bet she didn't look like that when she was getting screwed. Maybe she did. Maybe that's what turned her boyfriend on. This is the kind of horseshit I was thinking about. I don't know why I was seeing the world in such an ugly way, like stupid people and whores and scumballs and cretins and losers, but really, that's what I was seeing, just a parade of them, me going every other second, thank God I'm not like that asshole. I must have been nervous or something; sometimes *that* makes you see things a bit differently. Like everything could reach out and bite you on the throat.

Finally the doors shut and the bus pulled out on Bay. For the past little while, I'd avoided thinking about Scarlet, it was like touching a cold sore with your finger, just to see if it still hurts. But now, because I was going away, it wasn't so painful, now it wouldn't matter who she was with. And so as the bus pulled onto the expressway and picked up speed, I found myself thinking about her more and more, just these little moments, like when I found the teddy in her bed or her calling me up on those summer nights, me in my mother's room, feet dancing away on the wall. Boy, I shook my head, sure is incredible how things can change. I mean if you'd said to me then, you know on one of those nights when the fireflies went bopping around the garden window and my mother was out on the porch with a noggin, listening to "Arrivederci Roma," if you'd said Simon, in three little months all this is going to be gone and you're going to be on a bus heading south to Florida, school gone, house gone, Scarlet gone, I would have thought you were nuts. I mean just imagine what was going to happen in the *next* three months.

We drove along the highway, the tires making that haunting sound on the pavement, cigarette smoke drifting around; a fancy-dressed Italian man a few rows up turned on his little overhead light and was reading a book. I preferred to daydream though, just stare out the window and think about all the things ahead of me. I got out my wallet and went through it, item by item. Birth certificate, school card, fifteen dollars in small bills. E.K.'s envelope. From the inside flap where you're supposed to keep your driver's licence, I fished out a picture of me and Scarlet. It was the photo of us together in the booth that night down at the Exhibition. She was wearing a white shirt and a handkerchief around her neck, looking straight into the lens. I looked at it, I even smelt it. It had that Boucheron perfume on it, and it made my stomach wobble a little bit. I still loved her all right and when she heard about my trip who knows? And then, in spite of myself, I had this long daydream where someone phones her in Quebec, she's in boarding school and she takes the phone call in the basement, I can see her in her tunic, her hair in a pony-tail. It doesn't suit her, makes her chin look weak. Her skin looks a little yellow in my daydream. But still. Her shirt is open, it's a button-down and I can see her neck. That little dip in her throat. I can see her on the phone, someone is telling her I ran away. Really, she says, no kidding, he ran away in the middle of the night? He went to *Texas*? And then she goes back to her room, thinking what an *adventurer*! And then I'm looking out a window in Forest Hill, I'm looking up Dunvegan Road, it's snowy, just like in the Christmas cards and I see Mitch walking up the street, a little brown figure against the snow. And beside me, in the daydream, is Scarlet. We're sitting in this big house, it's very still, it smells great, like a Christmas tree and presents and parties downstairs. Just the way a house smells at Christmas. And the two of us are sitting there while the snow falls outside and you can't hear a thing through the windows.

I was thinking to myself that I was going to go travelling far, far away, maybe all the way to China, that I'd be gone for years and years and then, just when everyone figured I was dead and gone, I'd turn up again. Maybe I'd go to the seven wonders of the world, get a piece from each one, a stone or a blade of grass, and bring it back to Scarlet. That way she'd have to love me again.

Or maybe I'd volunteer for the French Foreign Legion. Fight in a war on the other side of the world; come back a hero. That way they'd have to forgive me for running away. I'd give a speech at my old school as the honoured guest. Look out over a whole roomful of kids and start with something like, "I remember when I used to sit out there."

No, on second thought, I wouldn't say that. Any time someone says that they always go on to bore you. They may remember sitting out there but they don't remember what it was like.

And on and on and on the bus went into the night.

Finally I felt us slow down, you could hear the engine whine in a most sorrowful fashion, and I looked out the front window and there, a hundred yards down the road, the border crossing, all lit up with signs and booths and flashing yellow lights and cars lined up.

"Would you get your paperwork ready, please," the driver said.

We pulled up alongside a booth, the doors opened and a man in a uniform and a hat came in. He started down the aisle toward me and I got so freaked out I wondered if I was going to just croak when he talked to me. I couldn't get my banging heart under control. He stopped for a moment, talking to three Indian guys near the front. Suddenly they got up and left the bus. I watched them go into a brick building, still clowning, like those guys who get thrown out of class all the time. The trip to the principal's office doesn't bother them a bit. They're used to it.

Then he was talking to the Italian in front of me, me feeling so uptight it was like I was wearing a mask and someone was tightening it from behind. Feeling like in another second I was just going to jump up and turn myself in, the tension being worse than anything that could happen, when he came over to me.

"Good evening, sir," he said.

"Good evening."

"And where are you going tonight?"

"Buffalo," I said.

"That's a good spot. Business or pleasure?"

I allowed myself a little laugh at his joke.

"Definitely pleasure."

"And how long will you be there?"

"About a week."

"Do you have any luggage?"

"Yes. A suitcase."

"And who will you be staying with?"

"I have a friend there."

"What's his address?"

"He's picking me up at the bus station."

"What's his name?"

"Ainsworth. Dick Ainsworth."

He paused for a minute.

"Do you have any identification, sir?"

I gave him my student card and my birth certificate. He handed me back the card. He studied the certificate for a second.

"How old are you?"

"I'm sixteen."

For some reason, he turned the certificate over, looked on the back. He tapped it against his thumbnail. He looked up and down the aisle.

"Would you follow me please, sir? And bring your luggage."

When we got inside, there was just me and the Indians. One of them caught my eye and came over.

"Got a smoke, buddy?"

I gave him one and then a couple more for his pals. I didn't want any problems but I didn't want to sit near those guys. They were trouble and I didn't want the customs guy thinking I was with them. In a little while he called me into a small green office. A metal table, two chairs, a picture of President Johnson in a plastic frame.

"That's a lot of luggage for one week, Mr Albright."

"Well, I'm an inexperienced traveller. I probably packed too much."

"Your parents know you're making this trip, Mr Albright?"

"Oh yes." I said it with a little laugh like we were all in on the joke. But he didn't smile.

"So if I gave them a call, they wouldn't be surprised to hear from me?"

"No, not at all."

"And you say your friend Dick Ainsworth is going to pick you up at the bus station?"

"Yes."

"Why don't we give him a call, have him pick you up here?"

"Well, I don't think that would be very nice," I said, like he was spoiling a good party or something. But needless to say that didn't bring him around.

"I don't know his phone number."

"Why don't you go over there and see if you can look it up."

Outside his office, just across the hall, were a couple of pay phones with phone books hanging from chains. I heard the Indian guys. They were jostling around in their seats like kids. Pushing each other. Their hair, which was black, was parted in the middle and fell all the way to their chests. They were very skinny, all of them in black jeans and black jean jackets. I wondered why they hadn't gone into the office first.

I went over to the phones and opened the phone book. I found a Dick Ainsworth, a few of them actually, and for a second, I could feel that fizzing again, and I thought I'd call one of them, explain my situation over the phone, persuade him to come down and get me.

"Listen," I'd say, "you don't know me but I'm a nice kid and

I'm in a bit of trouble here and I was hoping you could help me."

It was a bad idea. It was going to get me fucked. Why would a complete stranger come all the way down here in the middle of the night and smuggle a kid across the border? And if they caught me lying to them, then they'd really throw the book at me. They'd take me back to school in fucking chains. Thanks a lot, Scarlet, now look at the jam you got me in.

I wandered back into the guy's office. He was doing a ton of paperwork. He looked up and sort of raised his eyebrows, like he was going through the motions of wanting to know what happened.

"He wasn't there," I said.

He wasn't very surprised.

"Wait outside."

I went back and sat down. I heard the bus start up; a few moments later it pulled out. Just me and the Indian guys in a bright room.

We sat around for hours. I caught the customs guy's eye; I shook my head and smiled, like I was saying, if it wasn't for you, everything'd be cool. He didn't smile back. He was like a machine, that guy, just the worst sort of fellow to come across.

After awhile he came out of his office. Handed me a form, told me to sign it.

"What's happening?" I said.

"You're going home. And if you try to sneak back across this border, you'll be arrested."

We went outside in the dark and got in a bus. Half-full of sleeping people. Stuffy smelling. And then we started out. The Indian guys had run out of gas; they leaned against each other like busted deckchairs. I looked at my watch; it was five-thirty. By breakfast, they'd know I was gone. Arthur Deacon would ask someone where I was. Then someone'd ask someone else. It'd go around the room in whispers, "See Albright this morning? Where's Albright?" until it got to someone who knew. And then the whispers'd come all the way back across the room, "He fucked off."

"When?"

"In the middle of the night."

It'd come snaking back across the tables to Deacon. Being a responsible asshole, he'd get out of his seat, wipe his mouth and, looking very *gravitas*, approach the head table. By now, everyone'd know, everyone'd be watching. Deacon'd get to the head table, go around back, down he'd go until he got to Psycho Schiller. He'd lean over and whisper in his ear. Psycho, knowing he was being watched, wouldn't look up. He'd make a little notation on a pad and go back to his breakfast. Then after waiting a respectable amount of time, say a minute or two, no more, he'd get up and still not looking anyone in the eye, make his way slowly out of the cafeteria. Not long after that, they'd be sweating E.K., the headmaster in his beautiful suit and Psycho, E.K. crying, all red-faced, saying, "He went to Texas, he went to Texas."

And me, instead of hightailing it down south (I was fifty yards from total freedom), I was getting sucked back home. By recess I'd be sitting in the back of a police cruiser outside the main building, the fucking laughing-stock of the whole school. I'd even have to give the eleven dollars back. I'd be expelled. I'd be one of those guys walking across the quad, no one talking to me, everyone feeling sorry for me like I was a leper or something. And I wouldn't even have got a fucking adventure out of it.

We drove on and it started to get light. It was just the pissiest morning, grey sky, bits of rain, dreary, sad little houses every so often out the window. Telegraph poles going by. Wiping the fog off the window with the heel of my hand. More shitty little houses right smack in the middle of nowhere. I sat in the back of the bus, nodding like an old coot. It was like my brain was trying to escape into sleep.

The bus pulled off the highway and starting winding its way along a narrow country road. I sat up in my seat, looking around. Some guy was making getting-ready gestures up front. I looked at my watch. It wasn't even six yet but it was awfully fucking bright out. We pulled into a little town, very pretty with bright coloured stores, running alongside a river. The bus made that creaking sound and stopped outside a tiny station. Mist covered the windows. You couldn't see anything. The guy at the front of the bus got up to get off. The doors swished open. You could hear him go down. There was a moment where everything just hung there like a plate just about ready to fall off a table. The doors started to close again. I got up out of my seat. I hurried to the front of the bus.

"Where are we?" I said.

"Niagara Falls," the guy said.

I looked at him. He was staring straight ahead, waiting.

"Can I get out here?" I asked.

He turned and looked at me. He looked exactly like Danny Lang, the guy Daphne dropped me for.

"Do you live here?" he asked.

"Yeah."

"Then you better get out," he said.

The doors opened again. I got down. He got out after me and opened up the compartment under the bus. Pulled out my suitcase.

"What have you got in there? A body?" he asked.

A moment later I was standing alone by the river side, watching the bus pull around a corner and head back to the highway. I went over to my suitcase. I lifted it up onto the railing and spilt it over the side. It tumbled down into the green water with a splash. It hung there for a second, all my stuff, my jackets, my loafers, my school ties, my cufflinks, even my Grade Eight broad-jumping medal, it hung there for a second and then very slowly it started to revolve, it started to turn very slowly and head out into the middle of the stream, my brown suitcase full of all my stuff turning slowly and going south.

Then I started my way along the side of the river. I must have walked for about ten minutes when I came to a sign pointing towards the United States. Big arrow. I felt in my back pocket for my wallet. It was still there. I came across a narrow wooden bridge, I started walking across it. It was just for pedestrians. Dew on the wood. Very slippery. I crossed right over the river. I looked down for my suitcase but there was just the green water rushing underneath. I didn't stop though. Thought someone might be watching me. I could feel myself starting to freeze up. At the end of the bridge, maybe thirty yards away, was a little booth. I walked toward it, my intestines turning inside me. I got to the window. A man in the same uniform as the guy the night before slid open a window. He looked a little bit like Captain Kangaroo. As if he might have had a few drinks the night before and not be feeling so good but was being cheerful to cover it up.

"Good morning," he said.

"Good morning."

"Going across?"

"Yes, sir."

"For how long?"

"Just the day."

"Got any ID?"

"Sure."

He looked at my birth certificate.

"Oh, and this too," I said. I handed him my student card.

"Why aren't you in school today?" he asked.

It was the big one and it came screaming across the plate at a hundred miles an hour.

"A scholar's holiday."

"A what?"

"It's a scholar's holiday." I said it more clearly, looking him right in the eye and smiling the way I imagined someone with really good marks would.

"Okay," he said. He handed me back my stuff. I walked slowly down the gangplank and onto a street. I didn't look around. I put my hands in my pockets, looked up and down the street like a happy tourist and headed down the road. The road arched away slightly and after a few minutes, I peeked over my shoulder. I started running down the street. I heard a car horn honk behind me. It was a yellow Cadillac. I put out my thumb. The car pulled up alongside of me. The windows whirred down. Music boomed out of the inside of the car. It was that song from the dance last summer at Hidden Valley, "She's Gotta Move Up."

"Where you going, kid?" the driver asked.

"Florida," I said.

"Well, get in. I can get you started."

We were driving through town.

"It's a great thing you're doing, kid," he said. "I always wanted to do that. Just fuck off, you know. Wham! Gone!"

He drove me a few miles out to the turnpike, stopping at the foot of a huge bridge.

"Just stay on here kid, just stay on this route." He motioned to the bridge, this great big monster with cables rising up, the cars whizzing past us. "Fifteen hundred miles down that road, you're in Florida."

I got out. He gave me a honk and sped off back toward town. I started across the bridge. The wind was just howling. My hair standing on end. I could lean against the wind, it was so strong. I just walked on, getting more and more excited. I stopped about halfway. I looked down. The water roaring below, so far, far below me.

I made it, I thought, *I made it!*

Goodbye Mom, goodbye Dad, goodbye Upper Canada, goodbye Scarlet, goodbye Forest Hill, goodbye E.K., goodbye dormitory, goodbye Psycho, goodbye everyone. No hard feelings. Goodbye. Goodbye. Arrivederci Roma.

And then I started running along the top of the bridge toward the other side. The wind just whipping like crazy.

Except that's not what happened. What happened was I fell asleep on the bus back to Toronto and when I woke up we were pulling into the bus station down on Dundas Street. I just about jumped out of my pants. I looked at my watch. It was only seven o'clock. The Indians got out first but I just about pushed them down the stairs to make them hurry up. I grabbed my suitcase out of the hatch and flagged a cab. Told him to go like hell. We went up around the back of Upper Canada, me wide awake now, and I jumped at Kilbarry Road. I gave him a whopping tip.

I stuck my suitcase between the hedges and the school fence and shot up the back driveway. It was still raining and there wasn't a soul around. I went in the side door of the dormitory, up through the basement. You could smell the dust and the old pipes down there. I opened the door to my room. E.K. rolled over and looked at me. Funny thing is, he didn't even seem surprised.

"Jesus Christ," he said and rolled back over.

After awhile he scratched his shoulder.

"You owe me eleven bucks."

CHAPTER TEN

SNOW FELL. I was watching it flicker past my window. E.K. was sitting on the bed, pulling at that giant dong of his and cutting out pictures of some political guy from the newspaper and pasting them in a scrapbook.

"Hey, E.K.," I said, "did you know his girlfriend screws around? I met this guy that's balling her."

"Fuck you," he said, not even looking up.

The hall prefect came by. He had bowed legs and bad skin and for some mysterious reason he'd taken more or less an instant dislike to me. He came into the room without knocking, which was his way of showing contempt.

"Phone call," he said, grunting like a fucking Neanderthal, and then walked out again, clomp, clomp, leaving the door open, his fucked-up legs going down the hall in jeans. (Being a prefect, he was allowed to wear jeans after class. A real incentive to excellence, that one.)

I went down the stairs and into the phone booth and pulled the door shut. There was all this handwriting and gouging in the wood from all these kids doodling away with pens or knives or fucking machetes. I picked up the phone.

"If I stand on my tiptoes, I can almost see your room," she said.

The anaconda wrapped himself around my chest.

"Scarlet?"

"If you don't want to talk to me, that's fine."

"Well, whe . . . , where are you?"

"I'm just down the street. At Bishop Strachan."

I opened my mouth but nothing came out. My jaw just hung there like a busted lantern.

"I got expelled," she said. "I got caught smoking pot with a nun. Actually she was just a big lesbo from Los Angeles."

"Am I on the radio or something?"

"So now we're both in captivity," she said.

There was a bit of a pause while I picked at the wood with my fingernail, making a white groove.

"So I guess you heard," she said.

"What?"

"I broke up with Mitch."

"I never see Mitch. I couldn't pick Mitch out of a police line-up."

I heard another voice, an older woman's, at her end of the line. Scarlet put her hand over the mouthpiece and then in a moment she came back on.

"I gotta go," she said. "Don't think too shitty things about me, all right? Like you don't know the whole story."

She waited a second.

"All right, Simon?"

"All right."

"And don't tell anyone I called."

I went back up to my room.

"Guess who that was?" I said to E.K. I was pretty goosed up. In fact when I looked out the window, I noticed that everything seemed covered in a sort of magical glaze.

"Santa Claus," he said, snapping off a piece of Scotch tape and laying it carefully over something in his scrapbook.

I put my feet up on the desk. I put my arms behind my head.

"I wonder what she wants," I said out loud, not that I expected E.K. to pick up the ball. Since my trip to Texas, he'd been strangely uncurious about the comings and goings of my life. Odd that within a couple of months this guy, who was generally perceived as a cretin's cretin, was treating me almost like an equal, sometimes like an out-and-out nuisance. Which happens sometimes when people get to know me.

But later that night, just as I was getting into bed, some of the steam wore off and I thought to myself, something's wrong here, something is definitely wrong. It was like my subconscious was trying to tell me something but it wasn't quite loud enough, particularly with E.K. telling me about how he and his sister used to take all their clothes off and play perverto-man with the flashlight and stuff I'd rather not know about. But when something's bugging you, there's usually a pretty good reason for it, unless you're just nuts, and so once E.K shut up, which was after lights out, I started going over the conversation with Scarlet piece by piece. And after awhile it began to assume a "sinister character," if I might use an expression from my English class. Especially that *don't tell anyone*. When people tell you stuff other people aren't supposed to know, it's usually time to start sleeping with a revolver.

I was thinking to myself, fuck, maybe I sounded too friendly. Maybe I should have told her to fuck off. But then she might have. I started thinking about a whole lot of stuff, her kissing that prefect in my basement, giving me the axe only when she had Mitch back in the bag; and now telling me not to tell anyone she called. It was all sort of *sneaky*. Like she liked it that way. Preferred it that way. Take away the sneakiness and she's not so interested any more. There are some real shitty people on earth and it occurred to me that my former girlfriend, Scarlet Duke, might just be one of them.

But then I realized I didn't give a shit about any of that. I got all warm and sleepy and I thought, oh well, everything must be okay, otherwise I wouldn't feel so good, so cosy all tucked up here in my bed and falling asleep.

Next day I got out of bed with an unusual sensation. I had something to look forward to. I saw Mitch in the hallway just before prayers. He was hanging out with his gang of coolies, same bunch of war criminals as always. Normally I kind of slunk past these guys, hoping nobody would say anything to me. I usually had a little something prepared, some quick retort. That was the thing with those guys: if they weren't quite sure what you were going to come back with, they tended to leave you alone. But today I didn't find my heart speeding up when I got near them. In fact I felt a kind of weird kinship for old Mitch. It even felt a bit like affection; but I'm not stupid, I knew what it was. Now that he'd been kicked on his can, he didn't have it over me any more. I even had a terrible temptation to go over and say, "I heard from our little friend last night," just so him and his buddies would know. But I had a feeling that might be a little premature and I didn't want to look like an asshole twice. Moreover old Mitch didn't look exactly heartbroken. In fact he looked as if everything was hunky-dory. I wondered if he even knew he'd been broken up with. Hard to tell with a guy like Mitch. They're sort of like poodles, those guys. It doesn't take much to get them to wag their tails.

Later that night, when I was back in my room for study period, I heard the phone ring at the far end of the building and I thought, that's for me. I mean I wasn't hoping it was, I just *knew*. And sure enough, a few seconds later I heard footsteps coming along the hall and there was Mr Crater Face standing in the doorway.

"It's me again," she said. "Did you know it was me?"

"Course."

"I had a dream about you last night. I dreamt you took some girl back to my parents' apartment over on Chaplin. It made me really jealous. Why do you suppose I'd have a dream like that?"

"I have no idea."

"Do you ever have dreams like that?"

"Not that I remember."

"You're not hexing me are you? One of the girls here said you probably put a hex on me."

"Why would I do that?"

"Well, I wasn't very considerate, was I?"

"Oh hell, that's all over, Scarlet. People fall in love, they break up, big deal. Happens to everybody."

"You sound so blasé. Do you have a girlfriend? No, don't tell me. It'll just make me jealous. Don't you think it's strange though, me having that dream?"

I was cutting a groove in the counter with my nail again, brushing away the guck so you could see the clean white wood underneath.

"I've heard of stranger things."

She took a deep breath.

"I had to get him back, you know. I had to," she said. "A guy like you, you're probably above that stuff. But I'm not. I just had to *know* I could get him back. For awhile there, it was like he had like all the secrets to the universe."

"Mitch? Mitch can hardly find his way to the tuck shop."

"But you know what I mean. I mean I bet you wanted to

get even with Daphne Gunn. I bet if she'd given you a chance to, you know, even when you were with me, you would have taken it."

"Did you ever tell him, by the way?"

"About what?"

"About my aunt's house."

"I did, actually."

I suddenly remembered what Rachel had said about Scarlet staying out all night.

"Well, it doesn't matter," I said.

"It did to me," she said. "It was my first time."

"I thought you were with that folksinger."

"I told you. He just got it in part of the way. It didn't really count."

There was a silence.

"All the girls masturbate here," she said. "It's like a chicken coop at night."

"Jesus, Scarlet. No wonder you got expelled."

"Believe me, if you got expelled for that, there'd be nobody in the school. Do they put that saltpetre in your food?"

"Yeah. Tons of it."

"Doesn't do me any good," she said. "I must be oversexed or something."

"Oh really?"

"Sometimes I think the police are just going to come and take me away. Don't you think it's funny the way we can talk? You know, so easy. There must be a thread there or something."

"I don't know, Scarlet. Maybe."

"My father always said I should marry you. Right from the first time he met you. Shit," she said suddenly, whispering, "I have to go. Fuck. I'll call you tomorrow."

On Thursday night, my mother came down to the city and took me out to dinner. That was pretty unusual, going out on a week-night. She must have cleared it with Psycho, who was always sucking up to parents. All that pip, pip, pseudo-British stuff. (Now I knew what *pseudo* meant, I used it like every third word.)

We went to our favourite restaurant, that French joint. I was sort of excited, to tell you the truth. I had a feeling something was up, that there was something good in it for me. (Sometimes you can just feel your luck changing. Like opening a window in a stuffy room.) But I also had a feeling it would piss her off if she knew that, so I kept my cards pretty close to my chest. Finally she came out with it. Very understated, of course, but the fact was this; she couldn't stand living up north with the old man and she was splitting for awhile. Going to go down to stay with her old friend Aunt Marnie who had an apartment in Palm Beach.

"Are you going to get a divorce?" I asked.

"For God's sake, Simon, don't be such an alarmist."

When my mother was feeling guilty sometimes, she went on the attack. I didn't want her getting all jumpy like that so I said, "You know, ever since I was twelve I wanted you guys to split up."

That slowed her down a little bit. She lit a cigarette and very delicately nicked a trace of tobacco off her tongue.

"There's nothing final about this. All right? It's just for now."

"Will you get an apartment when you get back?"

"I don't know, Simon. I really don't. God's teeth!"

"That would be cool though, you know. I could come and stay with you. Better, I could come and *live* with you. Get out of boarding. God, that would be fabulous."

"Well, we'll just have to see, Simon."

And after awhile we started talking about other stuff, all sorts of things, Scarlet, Psycho, that time she went out with Errol Flynn.

"Did you know," she said, "they almost named me Mabel? The nun said to my mother, 'you've got five seconds to think of a name or we're going to name her Mabel.' And my mother said, 'uh, uh, Virginia.' It just *popped* out. Virginia Wolfe, that was my name. Imagine that. Ever since that play, people have been coming up to me at parties and saying, Who's Afraid of Virginia Woolf, Who's Afraid of Virginia Woolf. It's so *irritating*."

"So what do you say?"

"Oh, I just bare my fangs and smile and pretend I've never heard it before. I wrote a story for *The New Yorker* once, you know. It was published. It was quite good. But then I got married and . . ."

"To the race car driver?"

"Yes. Tommy. So handsome. But a drinker. He hid his bottles in our fireplace, under the ashes, and one day I found them and I just walked out of our apartment. And the next thing I knew, I was at a party over on St George Street and your father was there. Fresh back from the war. He was such a gent. That's the one thing about your father. He's a *gent*. There aren't many of those out there in the world. I know."

And when I looked at her, I felt something sink in my stomach. She still loves him, I thought. She's going to go away and she's going to miss him. She going to look around Palm Beach and she won't find any gents, not like him, and she'll come back. She'll come back to him and nothing's going to change. *Nothing is ever going to change.*

It started snowing early in the morning. The air all soft, these big snowflakes drifting by the window of Latin class, like somebody had had a huge pillow fight and all the feathers were slowly settling to earth. I lay with my head on my arms, old Willie Orr grinding on about the Gauls seizing and carrying off the Etruscan women and everybody kind of giggling until old Willie had finally had enough and he went over and cuffed some kid on the back of his dandruffy head and the whole class jumped like a herd of gazelles. And then everybody settled down again, the snow falling, Willie droning, the heating pipes going clank, clank every so often like some little man, way on the other side of the school, was smacking them with a crowbar. The wall clock went click, click and the arm jumped forward. One more minute gone. Sometimes, looking up at the clock, I'd get a wave of panic, like I was trapped in a car and we were going to keep driving back and forth across the same parking lot for eternity.

Anyway, finally enough Etruscan women had gotten seized and carried off for one day and we hustled out of Latin with that blast of energy you get at the end of something fatally boring. If you're not careful you can mistake it for having liked the class. But it's just relief.

By noon the back playing fields were covered in snow. A couple of Bishop Strachan girls walked by the main gates, their heads down, snowflakes covering their capes. You could see their bare legs underneath. And the long grey socks they wore up to their knees. Their legs always looked red and splotchy in this weather. Raw. Can't imagine how their teachers let them out of the school in such silly clothes. It'd be like my parents letting me wander around in shorts in the middle of the winter. Just before dark, there was this weird blue light that fell over the fields and schoolyard, downright biblical. From the second-floor window, I could see some little kid pulling his toboggan across the field, all done up in his snowsuit, scarf wrapped around his neck. A delivery truck made its way up the main drive into the school, sliding sideways and coming to a complete halt.

It just went on and on, the snow. It blew sideways; snow heaped up on the windowsills, on the stairs leading to the dining room, even on your eyebrows when you walked across the quad. It was like divine intervention. Going to fuck up everything tomorrow, the whole city was going to come to a standstill, half the dayboys wouldn't turn up, the teachers, seeing there was just half a class, would throw us a spare, let us talk. Always great, those days, a feeling like something different was happening.

Near nine that night I was back in my dorm, scraping a picture in the frost on the window with my fingernail; a balloon with two eyes and a smile and a long, wiggly string. If you didn't know better, you'd think I could really draw. But it was the only one I could do. This little genius guy with a brushcut, John Fraser, showed me how to do it years ago and I'd been perfecting it ever since.

Harper phoned.

"Listen," he said, "you gotta do me a favour. The old man called. I think he's freaking out a bit up at the cottage. The place is pretty fucking barren and he's been all by himself up there for like three weeks now. He asked me to go up and see him this weekend. I mean he didn't come out and say it, he just made some bullshit excuse that he needed me to help him with the storm windows. But I think he's lonely, and I can't go. I've got this chick I've got to see. Can you go? Just for the weekend. I feel kind of bad about him being up there."

"No," I said, "I can't. That's a whole weekend leave. That means I'd have to give up Saturday night next weekend. I can't do that. Not to go up there."

"Jesus, Simon, he really sounds fucked."

"Well, you go. I can't. Last thing I want to do with my spare time is spend it with that asshole."

"Great, Simon. Just great. Like you're so fucking selfish some-times I can't believe it."

"*I'm* selfish? Look who the fuck is talking. Here I am in San Quentin and you won't leave town because you want to get your wad sucked. And I am getting sick and tired of hearing that word, *selfish*."

"Well think about it anyway, will you? Just think about it?"

"Sure, I'll think about it. I promise."

And then I put the phone down and never gave it another thought.

For three days it snowed and it snowed and it snowed. And then one night, right after announcements, it stopped. Just like that, like flicking off a light switch. I opened the window and a pile of snow fell onto the floor. It was soft as grass though, soft and glittery. The moon hung in the sky and I could see my own breath. Suddenly my ears started ringing. *Somebody must be think-ing about you*, that's what my mother would say.

A little bit later, that bow-legged fuckweed was standing in my doorway, telling me there was a phone call for me.

"Some weather eh?" Scarlet said. "Doesn't it just make you want to go outside and *do* something? Roll in the snow. Steal something. Throw a rock through a window. Kiss somebody. It's so exciting. You know that sound, the sound cars make when they hit each other, that sort of *crunch*. God, I love that. That's a real winter sound."

At the top of the stairs I could see a pair of cowboy boots; the hall prefect was still there, listening.

"I think I got a bit of an audience here," I said.

The boots didn't move.

"All right," she said. "I'll talk. You just say yes or no. Do you have a roommate?"

"Yep."

"Is he a snitch?"

"Nope."

"Like if you snuck out, would he tell on you?"

I scraped out a groove in the wood with my thumbnail and then blew away the guck.

"Nope."

After awhile she said, "Because I've got an idea."

After midnight I slid open the window and dropped out into the fresh snow. E.K., having jerked off under the covers the usual six times, had fallen into his nightly coma. I didn't move. I stood there for a second, looking this way and that. A gust of cold wind blew, the snow all sparkly and exciting under the moon. I ran across the quad and stopped just before the entrance. I didn't want to run into Psycho coming back from walking his dog, this really ugly-looking boxer. It's true what they say, by the way: eventually dogs and their masters begin to look like each other. But there was nobody there. I hurried across the upper cricket pitch, the snow coming in over the tops of my shoes. I was a perfect target out there, under a full moon, running knee-deep in the snow. I felt like I was in a movie, running away from prison. Steve McQueen, one of those guys. Over my shoulder I could see the big yellow school clock, same one I remember looking at way up on the ferris wheel, the night Scarlet dumped me. Wow. Who'd have figured on this one?

Finally I got to the fence, these tall wooden pickets, just right for keeping out the barbarians. I followed them down till I got to the gate. It was frozen shut. I had to bang it a few times until it snapped open. I stepped out under the streetlights, then nipped across Forest Hill Road, past that house where that black-haired girl let me feel her up, and ran along Frybrook. At the far end of the street, maybe a hundred yards away, were the lower playing fields of Bishop Strachan. I headed toward them. I didn't even mind the cold on my feet. I turned up Warren Road and ran uphill alongside the playing fields and then turned in that little circular driveway where the little squirts get dropped off by the parents. I went over and gave the window a little push. I had to lean over the railing just a bit and when I did I caught a reflection of the moon. The window opened. I pushed it wide, checked over my shoulder and slid in head first, landing like a big bundle of laundry on the floor. You could tell, even in the dark, it was a classroom, the way it smelt, the dust, the chalk, the wood they make those desks from. And something else, too. Something different. I went to the door and peeked out. Sure enough, down the end of a dark hall was a big red exit sign. A fool couldn't miss it. So I went back into the classroom, took off my shoes, emptied out the snow and put them back on. Then I started down the hall, keeping very close to the wall. I heard a click, then another click; they must have had the same fucking clocks as the ones we had at Upper Canada. I looked up. Sure enough, there it was. Sometime past twelve-thirty. I got to the end of the hall and I started up the stairs. Very carefully, I climbed a few steps, then listened, another few steps, then listened, heart banging away. I could feel the air change, it smelt different there, like the bodies of sleeping girls. Like the way Scarlet's bedroom smelt, only a hundred times stronger.

I got to the third floor and I started along the hallway. A floorboard creaked, I mean it was like a shriek so I stepped over to the side, as far as I could get, my shoulder brushing the brick, and standing on my tiptoes I made my way down the hall till I got to the room with the red card. I opened the door. I heard a sheet rustle inside. I shut the door behind me.

"Is that you?" she whispered. "I never thought you'd come. I thought you'd chicken out."

I felt my way across the room and sat down on the side of the bed. For a moment everything was absolutely silent. The hall clock clicked again.

"Strange, eh?" I said.

"What do you mean?"

"Being here."

"Very."

"It smells nice."

"Yeah?"

"I like the way girls' rooms smell."

"You must have a sensitive nose. I can't tell the difference."

She didn't say anything else and I looked out the window. You could see a yellow light at the far end of the playing field.

"Who lives there?" I asked.

"Where?"

I took her hand and pointed out the window.

"That little house there."

"Oh there. That's the groundskeeper. He drinks. We stay away from there after dark."

She lowered her hand; it was under mine but she didn't move it.

"So are you still mad at me?" she said.

"I was never mad at you."

"You should have been."

"I wasn't."

"Honest?"

"Honest."

"I don't believe you."

Things got quiet again.

"I can hardly see you," she said. "Can you see me?"

"Sort of."

"I let my hair grow."

"Yes, I see that."

"Does it look French?"

"Yes."

"Not that it makes any difference in boarding school. You never see anyone. By the end of the term all the girls are wearing sweat pants anyway. It's the potatoes they feed you. Just like jail."

Just then, down the hall, a door opened and a pair of naked feet, you could tell by the sound, started down the hall in the other direction. The board shrieked again.

"See what I mean?" she whispered, "It's like a chicken coop in here."

"But why do they all go the bathroom?"

"Wash their hands, probably. They don't like the smell of it."

"Of what?"

"You know."

"Oh that."

"Some guys get up right after and go wash their hands. You know, like they've been working with battery acid or something."

"Sometimes you talk like a guy, Scarlet."

"That's because I'm part lesbo."

"Are you part lesbo?"

"Everybody's part something."

"I'm not part homo."

"Yes, you are."

"I am not."

"You mean you never played doctor when you were a little kid? Or jacked off with another guy?"

"Jesus, Scarlet, your mouth."

"But you did, didn't you?"

"No, I didn't. Never. Not once. Matter of fact, I had a friend once who took me down to his basement and asked me if I wanted to play doctor and I thought he was like mentally ill. I never liked him again. Jesus, what an idea."

"Well, that's very unusual."

"I don't think so."

The hall clock clicked again.

"Your pants are wet. I can feel them through the sheets."

"I should take them off."

She didn't say anything and a minute later, I got into bed beside her.

"Don't do anything, okay? This is weird enough," she said.

"I hope no one comes in."

"Don't even *say* that. I'm supposed to be on extra good behaviour. That was the condition for taking me. I had to swear on a dozen bibles I wouldn't corrupt anybody. Jesus! You're freezing."

"I'll warm up. God, this bed smells nice. Do all girls' beds smell this nice?"

"Don't talk so loud."

"What's that?" I asked.

"You know what that is."

"I mean what's it made of."

"Flannel. Very cosy. It was a Christmas present."

"Does it go all the way down?"

There was the sound of a flushing toilet and the naked feet came back along the hall. A door opened and closed.

"Do you ever see Daphne Gunn?" she asked.

"No."

"I saw her in the sport's shop yesterday. She was buying deodorant."

"I don't want to talk about Daphne."

"So what do you want to do?"

"Don't know."

She was quiet again. I could tell she was thinking about something.

"You won't be pissed off at me any more?" she said.

"No."

"Promise?"

She sat up, and in the moonlight I could see her lift it over her shoulders. I heard it land on the floor.

"Is that better?"

"Yes."

"Are you happy now?"

"Completely."

"This *is* pretty weird."

"Uh-huh."

"What are you doing?"

"Just getting comfortable"

"With your hand *there*?"

"Just for a second. I'm resting."

"Just resting."

"Yes."

"All right. But be careful. I don't want to end up in the hospital."

"I will be."

"No. Just there. And softer."

"Like that?"

"Yes. Just a little lower. Yes, that's it."

"Is that right?"

"Just keep doing that. Softly though. *Really* softly."

"How's that?"

"Perfect. Just don't talk for a second. Just keep doing it."

"Like that?"

"Shhh."

Then, after a bit, she sort of shuddered and put her hands over her face.

"God," she said, "I mean it, one night the police really *are* going to take me away."

The board in the middle of the hall creaked. Scarlet froze. We both listened. The board creaked again. But there was no sound, no footstep. She leaned over and putting her mouth very close to my ear, whispered, "Get in the cupboard."

I got out of bed, grabbed up my shoes and my pants, opened the cupboard and got in. A few moments later, I heard the door open and through a crack I saw the room fill with light.

"Scarlet?"

"Yes, Miss Jenkins?"

"Who are you talking to?"

"No one, Miss Jenkins."

There was a pause.

"Why is your nightdress on the floor?"

"I was hot, Miss Jenkins."

"Put it back on."

There was a flutter of material and then the sigh of a bed. Footsteps crossed in front of the cupboard. I looked at the floor. The window creaked as she unwound it.

"If you're hot, open the window."

"Yes, Miss Jenkins."

"Now go to sleep."

"Yes, Miss Jenkins."

I stayed in the cupboard for some time. Then very carefully I stepped back into the room. I went to the door and opened it and peeked out. The hallway was empty.

"All right," I whispered.

"Listen. Bring some string next time," she said. "The kind they use for wrapping parcels."

"What for?"

"You'll see."

It was algebra class, all those fucking brackets and little x's; I was sitting near the back, watching an icicle hanging from the outside roof. It was a big cone-shaped thing, gleaming in the morning sunshine, water dropping off the end of it, and I knew that in a few seconds or a few minutes it was going to lose its grip on the roof and come crashing down with a roar. And that's what I was waiting for.

There was a knock at the door and Harold, the messenger, came in. He was a nice old guy, always very polite to you in a way that made you polite back to him. He had this scanty white hair, a pink face, and he wore a blue uniform like a valet or something. All morning long he went from classroom to classroom delivering announcements from the headmaster's office, you know, like no ball hockey permitted in the parking lot, the southern soccer fields out of bounds until spring, that kind of thing.

"Good morning, Harold," the teacher said.

"Morning, sir," said Harold, always jaunty. "Albright to the headmaster's office."

There was a groan and some of the pricks in the class turned around, their eyes all bright with bloodlust. You could feel their creepy little peepers moving over your face, trying to see if you were scared.

I went out in the hall.

"What's up, Harold?"

"No idea, sir," he said and made his way down the hall, consulting his list. I took the stairs two at a time and hurried along the main hall. The principal's office was right at the end. The secretary, looking very fucking glum I might add, waved me through. When I saw Psycho Schiller there, I knew my goose was cooked.

The principal, a red-haired guy in his forties, took a few quick steps toward me. He was super pissed off, like about two seconds from hitting me.

"You have exactly one minute to tell me what you were doing in the girls' residence at Bishop Strachan last night and by God, Albright, if you lie to me, I'll cane your ass off right here on the spot."

You know the expression, pooping in your pants. That was the closest I ever came. I looked at his face, then at Psycho. No way out.

"I was visiting a friend," I said.

"We know that, stupid," he said, spitting out the words. "How many times have you been there?"

"It was my first time."

"Did you take anyone with you?"

"No."

"No, *sir*, you mannerless oaf!"

"Yes, sir. No, sir."

He stared at me hard for a second. I looked at the floor.

"The headmistress saw you, you fool. You left your bloody footprints all the way to the girl's room."

He turned to Schiller.

"Mr Schiller, do you have anything to add?"

"Not for the moment," he said. "I certainly shall after."

"Right. Now listen, you halfwit, you're going to march over to Bishop Strachan right now. You will go to Miss Jenkin's office, you will be on your best behaviour, you will apologize, you will take her step by step through everything you did, from getting in to getting out of that school, and then you will come back here immediately and we will decide what we're going to do with you. Understood?"

"Yes, sir."

"Now get out."

I ran over to the dormitory and got my coat, but on the way back I saw the strangest thing. You know these two guys, the principal and Psycho, like when I left the office, they were looking at me like they were measuring my neck for the noose, but on the way back across the quad I happened to glance up and I saw the two of them standing by the window. They were laughing. And I had a feeling they were laughing about this stunt, me getting caught in the girls' dormitory. It was like they had to act as if I'd done something really bad, you know, for my benefit, but between themselves, they must have figured it was just a fucking prank. I mean there's shit to get caught for and shit to get caught for. And stealing stuff or punching some kid in the mouth, that's another league. Even an asshole like Psycho must have known the difference.

Anyway I didn't spend a lot of time philosophizing on the relativity of crime, if you know what I mean. I sped over to Bishop Strachan, went in the side door and hurried along the corridor looking this way and that for the office. Scarlet was sitting in the hallway on a bench, white as a ghost. Before I had a chance to speak, she whispered, "Don't you *dare* tell them I left the window open."

"What?"

"I'll tell them you screwed me. I mean it."

I stared at her like she was a fucking stranger.

I went into Miss Jenkins' office. She was this stout, grey-haired woman with a big bosom. She called Scarlet into the room. Scarlet came in, looking very dark under the eyes.

"I am going to ask you some questions, Simon. And how you respond is very important to the safety of the girls in this school. Do you understand? There's a great deal more at stake here than just you."

"Yes, ma'am."

"How did you get in?"

"Through a window."

"Which window?"

"The Grade Nine window."

"How did you know it was the Grade Nine window?"

"I used to have a girlfriend in Grade Nine."

"Who was that?"

"Daphne Gunn."

She paused for a minute.

"How did you know the window would be open?"

Scarlet was looking at the floor, listening.

"I just took a chance."

"Did Scarlet leave it open for you?"

"No, ma'am."

"Are you sure?"

"Yes."

"Scarlet, is he telling the truth?"

"Yes, Miss Jenkins."

"Do you understand the significance of the question?"

"Not really, Miss Jenkins."

"If you didn't leave the window open, Scarlet, then what

your friend committed is a crime. Breaking and entering. I want you to appreciate this, Scarlet."

"I do."

"Well, did you at least *know* he was coming?"

"No, Miss Jenkins."

"I have to say to the both of you that I find this all rather unconvincing."

I didn't say anything. Scarlet was biting the inside of her lip and squeezing the tip of her index finger into her thumb.

"How did you know which room was Scarlet's?"

"She told me the number one time. I just remembered."

"There was a red card on your door, Scarlet. Was that for Simon's benefit?"

"No, Miss Jenkins. That was a reminder to do my history homework."

"Well, if you weren't expecting him and you didn't leave the window open, why did you let him hide in your cupboard?"

"I don't know."

Miss Jenkins nodded.

"Is there anything you'd like to add, Simon? Now's your chance."

"I'd like to say that I'm sorry for frightening you, Miss Jenkins. And I'm extremely sorry for all this fuss."

"Fuss is a peculiar choice of words, I must say."

She looked at Scarlet. "Well, I think I know everything I need to know. You can go back to your school now, Simon."

Just as I was leaving, she stopped me.

"How old are you?"

"Sixteen, Miss Jenkins."

She thought about that for a moment.

"All right. You can go."

I headed back over to Upper Canada. It was raining now, puddles everywhere, one of those death days in the city. I couldn't get that picture of Scarlet out of my head, those dark rings under her eyes, that little runt's face. It was like she'd turned into somebody else, like a completely unrecognizable stranger. Well, not entirely unrecognizable. I'd seen that look before. The night in front of her condominium when she gave me the axe. Whenever Scarlet wanted something that was going to cost somebody else their skin, she got this look on her face. First time I saw it, I thought it was an accident. But not the second time. No, that's what she's really like. And once you see what somebody's really like, you don't forget it.

I crossed over Dunvegan Road. I looked way up the hill. The trees were dying up there; somebody told me that. They had some disease and come springtime they were going to have to cut them all down.

Don't you dare!

Wow.

I got suspended that afternoon. Psycho called for a complete expulsion, I would have lost my year, the whole works, but the principal had a cooler head. I mean that's why he was the principal and Psycho wasn't. So I was out for three days.

I took the bus that afternoon. It was the milk run and we stopped in every little shitburg between here and Huntsville.

It was late, after eleven-thirty when I got there. Father was asleep in his chair in the living room. I stood there, looking at him for awhile. There was only a desk lamp on; the fire was out, the whole house very dark. Outside you could hear the melting snow dripping from the eavestroughs. And suddenly I remembered him driving me to the hospital once when I was little. It was the middle of the night and I fell asleep leaning against him. He rested his hand on my shoulder and I remember his shirt smelled of pipe tobacco and I found the smell comforting, like I was safe and being looked after.

"Dad?" I said. "Dad?"

His eyes opened and he got up, a strand of hair sticking straight up. He looked worn out.

"You're here."

"Yes," I said, "I'm here."

"Did you take a taxi?"

"Yes."

"I'm surprised he came down the driveway."

"I asked him to let me off up top."

"Very sensible."

I could see he was a little blurry-eyed and it occurred to me he was nervous; he'd been drinking because he was all freaked out about me coming. There'd be just the two of us in this big empty house in the dead of winter.

"The school called," he said. "Damn stupid business."

"I know."

"For Christ's sake, if you're going to do that kind of thing, don't get caught."

"I didn't. I got snitched on."

"Then don't do it with somebody who's going to snitch on you."

I followed him into the kitchen.

"Are you hungry?"

"A little. Yes. Always after a trip."

He made me a sandwich, badly cut and badly buttered, he was careless in the kitchen, rushed and impatient, but I was hungry so I gobbled it down.

"Have you seen your brother?"

"No," I said. "He's pretty busy these days, I hardly get to see him at all. Have you heard from Mother?"

He shook his head.

"Me neither," I said, which was also a lie.

"I hope you brought a good book," he said. "There's not much else here in the winter. Do you want a glass of milk with that?"

"It's all right. I'll get it."

"I made up the bed for you in your mother's room. We don't have to heat the upstairs."

"Yes. Good idea."

"Okay then. Goodnight, Simon."

"Goodnight, Dad."

He gave me a crisp little wave.

Some time in the night I woke up. I heard something moving around. A light went on at the end of the hall. I heard the fridge door open, then close. Footsteps going into the living room. I was going to lie there a few minutes longer and go see what was up. But I fell back asleep again.

It was a cheerful morning, sun on the snow so bright you had to squint. Icicles hanging on the house like glass. The water was really pouring out of the eaves now. It almost sounded like it was raining. There were even some bare patches of earth and the air smelt like warm ground. I put on my boots and went outside. You could hear our little stream running past in the ravine below. I used to go down there in the spring, when the ground was still wet, and stare into that stream and wonder *What's wrong? Why am I unhappy, is this unhappiness me?*

At the far end of the property I could hear a crow cawing. He cawed and cawed and then in slow motion he sailed up into the air, flapping his wings really slowly, and disappeared over the mountain.

I've never been a big one for country life, if you know what I mean, too much space, not enough happening, all those rolling hills going nowhere. It gave me a whiff of something out there, something I didn't like, and I came back inside and lit the fire. Just the smell of the wood, the crackling, made me feel better, less bleak. I don't know how anybody could live in that fucking house all by themselves. I would have gone bonkers. I made a note to myself to call Harper when I got back to town, tell him to get his face out of that chick's pussy long enough to go up and spend some time with the old man. Jesus, those fucking crows. Caw, caw, caw. It went right through your soul, just the emptiness of it.

That afternoon we drove over to Hidden Valley, sat in the chalet drinking coffee, watching the skiers. My father was normally a very snappy dresser, but today he wore a kind of crazy hat with flaps hanging down that made him look like a basset hound. A hat he wouldn't be caught dead in normally. But we had a nice time, shooting the breeze. Occasionally he couldn't remember stuff. I'd mention something, like something from last summer, and he'd sort of shake his head.

"No."

He said it a bit mechanically, as if he'd already said it quite a few times.

"Oh well," I said, "it'll probably come back to you."

"Let's hope not."

I looked over at him and realized he was making a joke.

"What was the name of your girlfriend in the army?"

"We called her the Mighty Atom. She was tiny with bright red hair."

"Did you love her?"

"No. Not really. She was married to a very decent chap. Flew airplanes. Crashed near the end of the war. They only found his boots. Damn shame."

"Were his feet still in them?"

"I don't know, Simon. I never asked."

Then he looked like he'd gone off somewhere. I was wondering if he was thinking about why my mother hadn't written.

Outside the window, an icicle broke free and crashed to the ground.

"I have to go to Toronto next week," he said. "I wish I didn't have to."

There was something odd about the way he said it, like it was a private thought.

"What for?"

"I have to have a skin treatment," he said. "It's not serious. I just wish I didn't have to go." Like the trip itself, the *hassle* of it, was bugging him more than actually seeing the doctor.

"Take the train," I said. "The train is much better. Classier. It's more of an adventure."

"Yeah," he said, still a little distracted. "Maybe that's what I'll do."

So we sat there for awhile longer, him wearing his silly hat, the skiers shooshing down the hill, some of them showing off, zigzagging here and there, all the way down to the bottom and then looking around real casual to see if anybody was watching. And nervous snowplowers going back and forth, their legs shaking with the strain.

Normally I like chalets. They're kind of sexy, girls in fabulous sweaters and black ski pants, their cheeks all rosy. I imagine they get up to some pretty sexy stuff with their boyfriends, you know, like later in front of the fireplace. There's something about those girls though, a kind of life I'll never have. I don't know what it is but I know it'll never belong to me.

Back at the house, the old man and I sat around in the living room, me reading some history of Australia I found in the basement.

"Can I put a record on?"

I expected him to say no, but I didn't *worry* that he'd snap at me.

"Yes," he said.

So I put something on, not real loud, but still in the old days he'd have sat there for thirty seconds and then told me to take it the fuck off. But he didn't. We sat there, him reading a biography of Rommel. At one point though, I looked around, I thought, God, this is weird, I wish Harper could see this. I mean here I am, on suspension, supposedly in like very big shit indeed and what am I doing? I'm sitting around in the living room of my cottage listening to "She's Gotta Move Up" with my fucking father. Very cool indeed. I should have got suspended earlier.

I don't know. It was like that weekend my father just seemed to give up on me. Like he finally came to the conclusion I wasn't going to turn out at all the way he wanted me to. But then again, maybe it had nothing to do with me, this kind of eerie peacefulness over everything.

He drove me to the train station the next day. It was a sunny day, cold, and he got out of the car and walked me along the platform. Carrying my little suitcase.

"I think I'll come back up next weekend," I said, thinking I might, but suspecting that by the time next weekend rolled around there'd be something else I'd want to do. Still I'm glad I said it.

"That'd be nice," he said. We gave each other an awkward little hug, I could feel the bristles against my cheek, like spiky sandpaper.

Then I got on the train.

He must have done it right after he got back from dropping me off at the station. My mom called him that night from Florida. There was no answer. She tried again the next day, all day, and the next morning she phoned the caretaker, a farmer who lived up the road, and told him to go in and have a look, break in if he had to. They don't know how he found the guns, but he used my brother's rifle, a .22 Cooey. It looks like a fucking toy. It really does. I suppose the length was right.

And they found a letter from my mother on the mantel-piece. Nothing in it, just chatty stuff, but I can't figure out why he told me he hadn't heard from her.

She flew home for the funeral. It was at Grace Church on the Hill, lots of people there. Then this long parade of cars took my daddy out to the graveyard; they said a few words over the coffin, and then it whirred down slowly into the ground. We went back to my Aunt Kay's after. She's just the most awful cunt in the world, bossy and a drunk. I caught her lapping up the booze in the kitchen; like she was supposed to be getting more hors d'oeuvres for the party but there she was standing by the sink, swigging it right out of the bottle. She was already in my bad books anyway. Back at the church, I was having a cigarette in the foyer with all the other men and when it was time to go in, when everybody was moving slowly toward the door, she rushed over and snapped at me, "Put that cigarette out!" like she was talking to a kid or something. I just gave her a look, like a real bad one and stood there, taking another puff, like I was daring her to do something about it. She fucked off plenty fast.

So she was extra careful with me at the wake, even though there was a part of me hoped she'd try to tangle with me. Funny. You'd think my mind'd be on other stuff but it wasn't. I really wanted to kick the shit of her.

Don't get me wrong though; there were a lot of nice people there, people asking me questions and making a big fuss over me. Harper stayed upstairs watching a game on TV. I went up to see him for awhile. He was wearing a brown corduroy jacket. He looked very cool.

"Who's playing?" I said.

"Somebody."

"Everything cool?" I said.

"Yeah. Cool. I'll be down in a minute. Listen," he said, "was the old man pissed off that I didn't go up there? Did he say anything?"

"Not a word."

"Are you sure?"

"Absolutely. Not a word."

"Because I keep thinking about it. I should have gone up there."

For once, I didn't have anything to say. We just both watched the TV for awhile and then I went back downstairs.

My mom was surrounded by people, and I had the funniest feeling she was sort of enjoying herself. I mean I'm not knocking her but all the attention, everything, a noggin in her hand, I just think she was having an all-right time. Being sad but in a sort of happy way. I don't know.

But I couldn't seem to settle anywhere, it was a bit like my party, I felt like I was looking for something, going in this room, going in that room, just sort of wandering around.

So I went out the front door for a cigarette, and I just kept going. I walked all the way down to the bus station and I bought a ticket north. I had to wait twenty minutes but that was all right. I sat in the back of the bus, puffing away. I was quite the smoker. Finally we took off, the tires making that swishing sound on the wet pavement. The bus was nearly empty; we stopped in Gravenhurst for awhile, but I didn't get down. I sat in the bus watching a fat lady eat potato chips inside the station. She ate the whole bag. And then we took off again.

It was a little after five when I got to the house, night coming down like chimney soot. I went in the side door. I went through the kitchen. I turned on the light. There was a shiny patch on the floor, right beside the table. That must have been where they cleaned up. He must have been lying right there. He must have been alive for awhile, the house getting dark, the phone ringing, the hall clock going tick, tick, tick.

I went into his bedroom. His suitcase was packed and beside the bed. He must have been getting ready to come down to the city after all. I flipped the suitcase onto the bed and opened it. The smell of him came right up at me. It filled the room. I picked up his hairbrush. I smelled it too. Then I slipped the suitcase down off the bed and pulled back the covers. I kicked off my shoes, and I got in. I arranged the pillow so I could lie just where his head was, where I could smell him the clearest. I closed my eyes. You could hear the whole house, the little creatures running around behind the walls, the furnace going on in the basement, like we were being looked after.

Did he hear that? Did he think about me? That I'd be sad and miss him? Did he think about us out there on the lake, the sun going down, letting out our fishing lines?

Did he realize we'd never see each other again?

Maybe he didn't think about me at all. Or maybe he thought I was just a little sparkle, right at the edge of things.

I'm just going to lie here a little while longer, I thought, I'm just going to lie here till I feel like getting up. And then I'll go back to the main road and put out my thumb and catch a ride. It's Tuesday. Somebody's bound to come along.